Lake Moobegon Days

Lake Moobegon Days

By Daniel J. Vance
Ilustrated by Robert A. Williams

AdVance Creative
PO Box 154
Vernon Center MN 56090

First Printing

ISBN 0-9672014-3-8

To Mark Littleton, my mentor and friend,
who encouraged me.

WELCOME!

Y̲ou'll read about rural Lake Moobegon in the pages ahead. For many of you it will bring back memories of your growin' up days. For others it may show you a new way to live.

But whatever you get from it, before you read any further, first flip back to the Appendix. Now up until recently I thought an Appendix was somethin' that got infected and burst like a water balloon and required loads of antibiotics but my publisher assures me it's a safe place to put information. So given that, back in that Appendix — it still seems strange saying it, like it's a body organ or something — I've included my address because I figure you might not be able to get all the good values you need from this book and so because of that you'll have to write and ask for more.

The stories ahead include some of my most favorite memories from the greatest best town in all these here United States. Hope you like it as much as I do.

Danny Talbott

ONE

Way back in the hills of southern Ohio but not too far back is a nice little town called Lake Moobegon. It's barely a blip on the map but it's still there, just a ten minute drive from Greenbush. Most people in Lake Moobegon are decent people who listen to Paul Harvey and country music, throw horseshoes, eat lots of sweets and love Jesus. Maybe they're a lot like you. But only you can decide on that.

The green and white sign along the James A. Rhodes Appalachian Highway outside town tells you, "CINCINNATI 48." If you take the Buford Road exit off the highway there and go south you're only a mile from town. Once you cross the town limits the road immediately becomes a Main Street that's not that different from most Main Streets: it's lined with a few nice homes, twisty oak trees, a few maples, and lots of smilin' people sittin' out front on their porches, wavin' at you as you drive by.

As you motor into town, on your left, after a few nice homes, you drive past the bright red cross of the Lake Moobegon Church of Christ, the Catholic Church, Ken's Barber Shoppe and Rudy's Beer Joint. On your right the only business you run across is the Cyclone Store, the local version of KMart, and it sits on the corner at the four-way stop, with its crumblin' white sign that has a picture of a cyclone on it.

The name "Cyclone Store" still puzzles folks. Most think it was named that because their prices were meant to tear up the competition but that's not what I think. "Cyclone" should refer to the way their clothing displays always look: messy. We'll never know the real answer behind the name thing because when the man who named it, Old Ben Dunn, died last year at 91 while fishing for crawdads, the name mystery died with him.

Across the four-way stop the road becomes South Main and the first business you come upon there is the pizza joint and its neon red sign featuring a picture of Possum Pete, the big Lake Moobegon legend. On that picture Pete's just eatin' his pepperoni pizza and smilin' big-like. Makes me laugh. Ha-ha. You can hear its screen door squeakin' open and bangin' shut almost all day and half into the night. They do business with folks all over and will actually deliver but for that you need to order a day in advance and buy a quart Pepsi with your pizza.

Further down South Main, on your left., you're now smellin' the dust from Cutlip Feed Mill, with its two big silos. It's sittin' along the B&O Railroad waitin' for trains to come by to drop off grain. The dust from the mill gets in your throat and eyes and makes you feel thirsty all the time. I suspect that's one reason why Possum Pizza has fared so well. The feed mill is the largest employer in town. It opened up after The Great World War that ended all wars. The Cutlips still own the mill and they are by far the wealthiest folks around.

Across the street from the mill you've got the town's nicest homes, three to be exact, the biggest of which is my friend Cliff's: The Lake Moobegon Rest-In-Peace Funeral Home. Actually it's his father's, but he's goin' to get it some day so you might as well call it his. It's one of those tall Victorian-types, the only one in town, and it's painted all gray with gray shutters so the mill dust doesn't show and they got a doorbell that buzzes and a little sign over the doorbell that reads, "FUNERAL HOME: DELIVERIES IN REAR."

So there you have it, Lake Moobegon, from north to south.

West to east is different. If you come into town that way you're travellin' Old Cincinnati Road and the first thing you see before crossin' the B&O railroad tracks is the glossy "Welcome to Lake Moobegon" sign. This used to be the main artery into town from Cincinnati before they built the James A. Rhodes Appalachian Highway that's now State Route 32. The glossy welcome sign states that Lake Moobegon is "Home of the First Ever Foreign Exchange Student in Hartan County History." Directly adjacent to the glossy welcome sign is the driveway to ClearView Apartments. ClearView has twenty units, was built in the '60s, and it houses folks who don't have their own spread yet. The units are real nice lookin' and all, with every apartment havin' restrooms, but I do hear tell you have to go into the Suds Yer Duds place in town to do laundry. That's not too bad of a thing if you can only find a dryer there that works. If you keep movin' on Old Cincinnati Road towards town you'll finally cross over the B&O railroad tracks, bump, bump, with Tex's Convenience store on your left and and on your right Cutlip Dairy Whip — the place with the freshest jimmies around. The Cutlips own the Dairy Whip, the feed mill, and some say the Methodist Church. They live across the street from the Dairy Whip, in the Cutlip Mansion, next to Tex's, and it's a huge place with double doors and probably half a dozen rooms. The Cutlips have the only in-ground swimming pool in Lake Moobegon and are kind enough to let Eastern High School use it for graduation parties.

Next to the Dairy Whip and conveniently located across the street from the Cutlip Mansion is Lake Moobegon Town Hall. Havin' the Town Hall near the Cutlips wasn't an accident. Since 1916 the town hasn't had anyone but a Cutlip as mayor. Like I said, the Cutlips run Lake Moobegon but that doesn't seem to upset anyone. Someone has to do it. Even after all these years the town still feels it owes the Cutlips for bringin' the feed mill to town. The townspeople have always been a mite antsy because they're afraid the Cutlips might up and move to Pickle's Cove and boy would that be an awful blow to the town's pride. I think we look at the Cutlips bein' mayor as insurance. The feed mill brought prosperity and is probably the reason Lake Moobegon is still referred to in the AAA Triptik as "Queen of White Oak Valley."

After the Town Hall you S-curve through what's left of town, a couple of run-down homes on your right, another on your left, more oak trees, and then there's the white vinyl-clad United Methodist Church on your left. The Methodist Church hosts the Lake Moobegon United Methodist Church Annual August Ice Cream Festival (L.M.U.M.C.A.A.I.C.F.), one of the more important events on the Lake Moobegon social calendar. It's also home to Rev. Otto Milroy, one of the county's largest preachers and a rabid Pittsburgh Pirates fan. Took folks a long spell to get used to a man of God actually rootin' for someone other than our beloved Reds.

Across from the Methodists you can hear the hair dryers whirrin' at Monica's Hair Loft where Madge runs the show. She inherited the place from her Aunt Monica and does a real nice job and has prospered primarily due to money spent there by the Cutlip women. The runnin' joke in town is that the Cutlip women live at the Hair Loft and the men live at the town hall and it's a wonder there's any little Cutlips.

11

Years ago when I was young, I'd bike past Monica's Hair Loft and have to hold my nose to block out that terrible "perm" smell. A few years back I walked by — this time after the Methodist Ice Cream Festival — and lo and behold that same smell was lingerin' in the air. Probably the same people gettin' permed, too. Things don't change much around here. I can reconstruct a typical beauty shop conversation in my mind even now.

"Why, Edna?" says Mary Lou. "Did you hear what I heard?"

Edna's in a panic because there's somethin' Mary Lou knows that she doesn't. "What you hear?" she asks while hiding her curiosity with a scrunched up *Cincinnati Post.*

Mary Lou mumbles into her hand. "You must not a heard, Edna, or else you'd a knowed what I was talkin' about."

"Talk louder," Edna yells into the paper, trying to get her friend to blab it all to the rest of the beauty shop. "These hair dryers make such a commotion!"

At the four-way stop, this time from the west (not the north), is where Main Street meets Old Cincinnati again, and you can see the brick side wall of the Cyclone Store, this time on your left, with its crumblin' white sign on this side that tells you to "S VE B G." After you've finished gawkin' at that and tryin' to figure out the missin' letters — and it is an ugly sign — then cross the four-way stop but be careful because John Deere tractors will sometimes run right through without stopping.

Now that you've crossed the intersection, the first building on your right is the three-story brick-and-block Lake Moobegon Farmer's Bank and Trust Building. Inside the bank it's dark and cold and the place echoes because it has marble floors. This is where town gossip gets spread by Brian The Head Teller and Alverna The Assistant.

Some people don't subscribe to the county newspaper, *The News Democrat*, circulation 2118, because they get all their news from Brian and Alverna. It's amazing what these two can come up with. If the Cutlips ever thought of leavin' town ol' Brian and Alverna would know it even before the Cutlips. And the big tradition is sendin' a pregnant woman to Farmer's Bank to find out if her baby's male or female. Brian and Alverna are right 75 percent of the time.

Ellis Shaw Real Estate, which is across the street from the bank, has recently had a major uptick in business. Cincinnati folks are beginnin' to leave that city because of crime and drugs and one place they've been lookin' at is Lake Moobegon. With all our cultural activities it's right natural we'd get some attention. Ellis has been sellin' real estate in Lake Moobegon for 25 years and if you walk in his front door right now you just might be able to hear him sellin' a City couple on the benefits of Lake Moobegon.

"What is there to do around here?" asks the prettied-up young City woman smellin' like a spilled bottle of French perfume. "I like the quiet atmosphere, the land's cheap, but what will my children do for entertainment?"

While Ellis smiles at her real long in order to think up an answer, her City husband, wearing a gold chain around his neck, is starin' out the side window towards the four-way stop where a '56 Ford tractor is pullin' up with ol' Johnny Bachmann on it. Johnny has a killer wad of Red Man chewin' tobacco puffin' out his cheeks, and tobacco juice is dribblin' down his chin in a heavy stream onto his Wranglers. Johnny waves at the City man, but the City man doesn't wave back.

Ellis touches his cheek as the City man turns towards him. "Folks, you're not going to believe all the hidden entertainment gems we got here in Hartan County," he says. "Why, just in Lake Moobegon alone we got the Lake Moobegon Fourth of July parade that happens every year on the fourth of July. It's the talk of Hartan County and rivals anything in Cincinnati. Then we got the Methodist Ice Cream Festival."

"Oh, really?" she says, her eyebrows archin' real big-like. A funny grin cracks the man's face, like he can't believe it all.

Ellis continues dutifully, yankin' on his index finger with each new attraction that rolls off his lips. "We got Little League for boys; White Oak Creek for salamanders; the Girl Scout troop at the Baptist Church. Your husband can even be part of the Hartan County Church Softball League. You are saved, aren't you?"

She squinted her eyes to a slit. "Saved?"

"You know, born again?"

The woman looks at the floor, picks lint off her pants. She mumbles a few unintelligible words. She laughs nervously. "If what you mean is whether we belong to a church or not, yes, we do belong to a church."

Ellis says, "We got five churches in town and another five within ten minutes."

"And what do you folks do on Saturday nights?" asks the City man, chuckling.

"Remember the road you came in on?"

The City man nods.

Ellis wags his index finger north. "That's the James A. Rhodes Appalachian Highway," he says, "and it's the main travellin' artery for folks goin' from Cincinnati to West Virginia. I get a lot of my entertainment by lookin' for out-of-state cars. We all pretty much like sittin' on the hill overlookin' the Gas & Go and watchin' with binoculars as the folks drive up. Billy Fender holds the record for furthest away plate: he spied one from Idaho. Tammi Jones found the plate with the weirdest saying: Missouri, with "Show Me." It's my favorite weekend activity, watchin' the cars. I'm still waitin' for the day when I spy one from Alaska or Saskatchewan."

"Oh. That's nice." The City man and woman then make dead fish eyes at one another, get up, leave Ellis, and drive Main Street towards the highway. They don't even say goodbye, but that's big-city manners.

Some people just don't appreciate what the Lake Moobegon and Greater Hartan County Metro Area have to offer. I've heard people say Lake Moobegon is way behind the times but Lake Moobegoners like to think they're so far behind the times they're actually ahead of them. After all, history does tend to repeat itself and everyone figures before long more folks caught in the rat race will be lookin' this way. A modest lifestyle has its benefits.

Now that we're done with Ellis — quite a salesman, ain't he? — just squeak-open the front door to his real estate office, make left and navigate the crooked sidewalk up Old Cincinnati Road. Across the street next to Farmers Bank is Billy's Sub Shop and its new sign. Next to that is Lake Moobegon Drug Store with a real pharmacist (unlike the one in Greenbush that sells just counter medicine) And next to that is Lake Moobegon Pool Hall and Social Club.

On the same side of the street you're on now, the business nearest Ellis is Suds Yer Duds Laundry where the dryers don't work and then you got Shorty McGuire's Auto Repair Shop where Shorty sometimes forgets to open the windows to let his exhaust fumes escape. The only other businesses on that strip are Gas & Go, out further, and the abandoned creamery out further than that. Of course I can't forget Fender Brother's IGA Grocery which sits by the old creamery because they'd kill me if I forgot to mention them. (They like free advertisin'.)

All in all, Lake Moobegon is a right nice place, not weighed down with the shallowness you often find in The City. Folks around here like their lives plain and simple and that's probably why they eat so much vanilla ice cream and animal crackers.

TWO

Lake Moobegoners refer to Cincinnati as "The City" and they go into The City to watch the Reds play or they car pool there for work, which is about all the usefulness they have for The City otherwise they'd live there. They like clean air, lots of acreage, friends and the Slow Life. All 787 residents of Lake Moobegon like it that way.

"Well, what you want to do tonight?" asks Dad, sweatin' up a storm.

Mom tosses her well-worn TV Guide towards the kitchen and itches her lower lip with the nail of her pinky finger. "As I see it we got a good many options," she says. "First, we could sit home and watch T-V. I hear there's a right nice country music special on tonight. Johnny Cash's supposed to warble."

"Uh-huh," mumbles Dad as he nods and stretches his legs out on the new plaid ottoman he bought at the Tuesday night auction in Greenbush. He's not a big Johnny Cash man at all. More like George Jones.

Mom chatters on. "Or we could go down to the Gas & Go and watch the cars come in. Jimmy Perry saw one from Wisconsin yesterday."

"Well?" Dad scratches his temple, frowns. He isn't sold.

"Or we could take a drive to the river and back," she says. "Suppose to be a nice night tonight and we could take a look at how well Grandma's tobacco is growin'. And then, too, Paul Harvey'll be on in twenty minutes."

Dad slaps both hands onto his knees. "That's the clincher!" he shouts. His eyes are beginning to glisten at the thought of hearing Paul Harvey. "And maybe we can stop in at the Dairy Whip on the way back for a vanilla cone with jimmies."

"Sounds like a winner."

So Mom and Dad gather the kids and head for their definition of a perfect evening. Dad presses the pedal on his weighty eight-cylinder Plymouth while seated alongside her and little Billy. The three older boys are in the back soakin' up all the excitement. The family does a drive about once or twice a week in the summer when the weather is hot and there isn't much breeze.

Dad motions towards a barn off to his right. "Well, looky there," he says. "It looks like Judd Rose done got himself a new combine. Bet that cost a pretty penny."

"Brian down at the bank told me he bought it with a huge loan," says Mom, tryin' to smear Blistex all over her cracked lips while the car slides back and forth across the gravel road.

Dust from the gravel is creatin' a cloud in Dad's rearview mirror. "Got to be careful nowadays takin' out those big loans," he says. "You never know if you can pay 'em back."

In the back seat the three older children are suffocating because Dad forgot to roll the windows down yet again. There's a reason why he "forgets." A long time ago, when Dad was but a teenager, he would stick his head out his father's Edsel window because he liked makin' those funny noises with his mouth — you know, the kind of noise you make when you blow into an empty Pepsi bottle and it sounds like a musical instrument? Dad used to be able to do the same with his mouth while he was flyin' down the road in the Edsel. He always said 45 m.p.h. was ideal speed. It made a G-sharp tone, he said, or a B-flat, dependin' on humidity or the wind direction.

Well, he really liked doin' that and all — and would have continued doin' it to this day probably — except for an incident when he was a 15-year-old that happened south of the feed mill down Hamer Road. To hear him tell it, he was makin' a nice B-flat pitch with his mouth wide open when a horsefly zoomed right in and down his throat and into his stomach. Scared him half to death. Since he didn't know what he'd swallowed — could have been a diseased barn swallow or worse — they rushed him to Hartan County General Hospital where a doctor laid him up on the emergency room bed nearest the water cooler.

Dad said the entire medical brain trust of Hartan County was there that day, what a frightening thought, and you could hear their brains clickin' and whirrin' in tryin' to decide what to do. At the time Dad didn't know what had flown in because he'd always closed his eyes while makin' the noise because when he kept them open his eyes would water so bad he couldn't see. The doctors ended up leavin' whatever it was in there — they believed it to be a horsefly but weren't totally sure — and to this day Dad makes his children suffer through the first mile before they have to remind him to roll the windows down.

"Dad! Windows!"

"Okay," he shouts back as his left hand begins makin' rapid circles with the window crank.

"Mommy, I need to go to bathroom," whines Little Billy, who is about an inch short of the first bolt on a John Deere tire, just a wee little thing.

"Why didn't you tell us that back home?"

"I didn't have to go then."

After a pit stop at Gas & Go, the drive continues. The breeze feels stiff on Dad's hot, parched neck. He's workin' up a pretty big thirst just thinkin' of the Dairy Whip and vanilla cones and jimmies. In the rearview he sees his boys soakin' in the wind, lookin' side to side, watchin' the soy beans and tobacco grow, and he knows they're probably thinkin' about vanilla cones and jimmies, too.

Up a ways is Grandma Renie's farm. Her tobacco plants have just been planted — actually replanted — into the field behind the sheep barn. Before long she'll have to chop the tops off and before you know it harvest will come. Contrary to what you might think, tobacco is a healthy cash crop in southern Ohio.

"You think Grandma's gonna need help toppin' this year?" asks Mom.

"Don't know," says Dad, itchin' his neck. "How 'bout if we ask her."

Right then Dad jerks the steering wheel right and leaves the main road all of a sudden to drive up Grandma Renie's front lawn, *bump*, *bump*, *bump*. Her house sits a far piece back, the yard is bumpy, and if you were watchin' from a distance the childrens' heads would be bobbin' up and down like the heads of those plastic football men you sometimes see on car dashboards. Few folks in Lake Moobegon have much use for paved driveways in the summer.

Dad honks his horn. "Grandma? you home?"

A set of window shutters creak open. Grandma is there with a faint smile, a pleasant but ornery smile, and she's runnin' her fingers through that lily-white hair of hers. "Why, is that my son?" she asks, squinting because of the low evening sun. "So they finally let you out of prison?"

Dad isn't amused. "Ha-ha," he deadpans. "Won't you quit it with that prison line? We were just out takin' a drive and thought we'd stop by. Is there anything wrong with that?"

She says, "Make it quick. I got rhubarb pie in the oven, taters boilin' and Paul Harvey. Better talk fast." Grandma closes her shutters halfway as if to reinforce her point.

"You gonna need us to top the 'backy this year?" Dad asks.

"Probably not," she replies. But I do need help hangin'. That's heavy work and you know how much I hate those tobacco worms."

21

Dad nods. "We'll help you with the hangin'."

"Thanks," Grandma says, biting her lip. She wrings her hands and looks off into the distance, as if she's remembering a sad scene from her past.

Dad senses it, so he thinks about closing down the conversation. There will be time to learn what's wrong when he stops by the following day to drop off her heart medicine from the pharmacist.

"Sorry to bother you. Didn't mean to interrupt," he says. "Suppose we better mozy on to the Dairy Whip."

"Thanks for droppin' by."

Dad jerks the transmission lever into gear to accelerate. Of course, he'd never left the car during the whole conversation. He'd been talkin' to her with his window rolled down and she'd been talkin' to him through the shutters. Folks here do that. 'Bout the only times they don't do it is if the weather's snowy or rainy which tends to mess up the yard or else they're on an extended visitin' trip and want to sit down inside to drink lemonade and eat strawberries with sugar sprinkled on top.

On the way to the Dairy Whip — and with Dad still thinkin' about Grandma Renie's bout with lip biting and hand wringing — Little Billy breaks what had become an awkward silence. "When do we get some ice cream?"

"Hold your horses young feller," Dad says, giving the Plymouth some gas as they round the curve near Trent's cow barn and Wardlow Road. "We'll be there in two shakes of a stick."

One of the boys in the back says, "I'm gonna get me one of those banana boats with a butterscotch top."

"Oh, no, you're not, young man." Dad narrows his gaze to stare down the overly hungry boy in his rearview. "We're gettin' cones; Jimmies if you want 'em. We can't afford banana boats, that is, unless you want to work for Mr. Cutlip at the Dairy Whip to earn yours."

The boy curls his lips. "That's quite all right, Dad."

For all intents and purposes, the Cutlip Dairy Whip has been the social center of Lake Moobegon for years. It was even the hang-out for teens until the Carsons of Pickle's Cove built the Aut-O-Matic bowling alley that didn't need pinsetters.

Standin' proud inside the Dairy Whip is Kathy Cutlip and she's real pretty with her black hair up and tied with a red ribbon. One thing about the Cutlips, they always keep up their personal appearance real nice.

23

"How do?" says Dad, wavin' his palm at her.

"How do, Mr. Talbott." answers Kathy as she leans across the counter with a monster wad of bubble gum puffin' up her cheeks like she's some kind of gray squirrel filled with nuts. "What can I, *chomp*, do you *chomp*, out of?"

Dad glances at the menu board but really doesn't have to because he knew what he wanted even before the trip began. It's been the same for the last seven years or more. "I suspect we'll have five vanilla cones with jimmies and one chocolate cone with an Oreo cookie on top for Little Billy."

After a few minutes of intense work in the backroom, Kathy does it up just right.

"Mmmm. Sure is good!" gushes Dad after takin' his lick.

"You bet!" agrees Mom as she turns to face the boys in the backseat. "Now don't get that on your clothes," she reminds them. "Use your napkins."

"Yes, Mother."

Dad throws the eight-cylinder Plymouth into gear and slowly begins to roll home after another drive over the gravel roads that run alongside Lake Moobegon's tobacco and corn fields. One of the boys in the back forgets to use his napkin and ice cream falls on the seat next to him. He tries to cover it up with his leg so no one will notice.

My time flies. It seems like this drive with Dad, Mom, and my three brothers happened yesterday when in fact it was 25 years ago. I can still taste the thick dust from the gravel and feel the push of the breeze as it hits my face. Folks in Lake Moobegon still take drives and I suppose they always will.

I miss those drives.

THREE

The Lake Moobegon Fourth of July parade goes right down Old Cincinnati Road and ends up at the Lion's Club Park on the east end, out past Fender's Grocery. This event solidifies Lake Moobegon's reputation as "Queen of the White Oak Valley."

The Fourth of July parade is the only one of its kind and folks from far away as Greenbush and Pickle's Cove stop to see the sights. One year a family drove up from Maysville, Kentucky, after they'd read about it in a *Hartan County News Democrat* they'd found covering the floor of a used car purchased in Riplet. I think their expectations were a mite high given the excitable write-up in that paper by Tommy Givens, who always has to impress people with the fact he's taken not one but two creative writing classes from the University of Cincinnati Raymond Walters Branch.

The father of that Maysville family was overheard to say he didn't like Possum Pizza's Ground Hog Pizza, so they haven't been back.

This year's Fourth of July celebration was one of the best in recent memory. Johnny Lee Crawford — that's Johnny Lee Crawford on Mill Road, not his cousin from Martin's Sink — finally won the Fourth of July parade float contest with his version of the Statue of Liberty that sits in New York harbor. He'd been tryin' to win the float contest for the last ten years and it had become nigh an obsession for him.

Get this: He stood his cousin Betsy Crawford in an old Radio Flyer wagon and dressed her up with robe and torch and had her pose like she was reading from a book. Just like the real Statue of Liberty.

I can still see ol' Johnny Lee gallivantin' up Main Street, pullin' pretty Betsy in that there wagon. It was a sight to behold. Betsy's hair was done up real nice by Madge from Monica's Hair Loft and she had on a prom dress that was made out of one of those French fabrics I can't pronounce even after hearin' someone say it for me. There was a bright red corsage pinned to her dress but because of the heat the poor corsage wilted halfway through and looked like a dead fish near the end.

And Johnny Lee? Well, he was all smiles and giggles as he dragged Betsy along that parade route, knowin' his Statue of Liberty float was the artistic masterpiece of the parade and envy of all other float entrants. They so impressed the judge, Mayor Cutlip, that Johnny Lee and Betsy won the Mayor's Award, which was a ten dollar gift certificate to Cutlip Dairy Whip.

To make things look super genuine-like, Johnny Lee had paper-mached around an acetylene torch, making it look like the real Statue of Liberty torch. It had a blue flame and everything and it made that hissin' noise acetylene torches make. We all think that's what swung the decision in his favor.

After they got the Mayor's Award, Johnny Lee and Betsy sat down in front of Farmer's Bank at the four-way stop to bask in the glow of victory. A dream come true for ol' Johnny Lee. And that's where I saw him, clutchin' that gift certificate and smilin' wider than a pig in slop.

Then Betsy did a stupid thing and sat the acetylene torch with the flame pointed up while he adjusted her hair. Before you could say Jackie Robinson that torch was lappin' at the fringe of Betsy's prom dress and it caught fire. Uh-oh.

Talk about an event. Betsy was squealin' like a greased pig and runnin' in circles and of course all her excitement just fanned the flames higher. Johnny Lee tried jumpin' on top of her to put her out but by then the flames had really taken a likin' to that French fabric of hers and then he started yellin' and screamin' because he was gettin' burnt and everybody was yellin' and screamin' because they were both gettin' burnt. A real nightmare. I'd never seen such a thing.

Fortunately for Betsy the town fire truck circa 1948 was two floats down. The firemen heard the screams and rushed over. Everybody was real nervous because the volunteer firemen hadn't had that many chances to fight real fires and you could see the worried looks on everyone's faces as they drove the truck over with the siren blarin' and the fire dog, Chuck the Bassett Hound, with his nose pressed up against the windshield glass.

No need to worry, though. All it took was two squirts to put her out. She looked sad standing there wet with part of her prom dress toasted and half the town feelin' sorry for her but if you ask me it was a lot better than gettin' burnt for good.

Quite a few folks said it was Betsy's fault because she shouldn't have been playin' with fire. I seem to think it was Johnny Lee's zeal to win the gift certificate that got them burnt. Fortunately, Johnny Lee has since realized how stupid he was for usin' a real acetylene torch and has apologized to Betsy for his greed.

FOUR

Another event in Lake Moobegon but not as big as the parade is the Lake Moobegon United Methodist Church Annual August Ice Cream Festival (L.M.U.M.C.A.A.I.C.F.) held every year since the Great War that ended all wars: WWI.

The Methodists make better ice cream than the Presbyterians. In my opinion, their best flavors are vanilla and lemon sherbet. I particularly like the lemon sherbet because it tastes so lemony. This year they attracted a couple hundred people and it was an opportunity for folks that had moved away to return home and meet old friends.

My Grandma Renie has a love/hate relationship with the L.M.U.M.C.A.A.I.C.F. She loves reminiscing with folks from her generation but lately that's fewer and fewer and that's why she hates it.

She has been the oldest living graduate of the Lake Moobegon High School Class of '20 for a few years. (That's way before they merged Lake Moobegon with Winlister and formed Eastern High School from the two.) Grandma says her only remaining goal in life is to be get a true-to-life signed congratulations from the President of the United States of America on her 100th birthday.

Let me tell you about last year's festival.

Florie Estes, a woman almost 90, walked up while Grandma and I were seated on folding chairs on the Methodist back lot near the forsythia bushes.

Florie fluttered her eyes like a song bird. "Well, Renie, how you doin', dear?"

"Still kickin'. They ain't put me in the grave yet," said Grandma with her usual greetin' as she pressed a soothing dish of vanilla ice cream up tight against her forehead. "Had a bout with the flu but feel better now. You know what that flu's like when it hits. It hits uglier than a big green tobacco worm."

Florie nodded. "You're tellin' me? Hit me last December and knocked me out terrible. Was yours one of those where you get a fever and it lingered or did it go right away?"

"No, deary, it stayed to visit. Must have taken a likin' to me."

"You get a fever?"

Grandma rolled her blue eyes, inched forward in her seat. "Get a feee-verrrr? Land yes! Went to one-oh-two before the doctor poked a fork in me. Was decked out on that hot davenport for a good three days. Life squad came and took me to Hartan County General before it got too bad."

Florie wondered. "Why didn't he send you to The City?"

"Guess he figured I'd be whiter than bleached flour if we'd made that long drive," chuckled Grandma, her belly jiggling like a bag of Jell-O. "Wouldn't even have had to embalm me."

"Must been bad."

Here it was, a pause in the conversation, so I made my move to get Grannie home. It had been a long day. "Grandma?" I whispered. "When we leavin'?" I nudged her elbow with a sherbet spoon.

While Florie listened in with a grin, Grandma said, "How 'bout now. It's as good a time to leave as any." She turned to Florie. "No offense deary but it's time for this old body to head to the barn. It's awful hot out here and I do have the flu. Hope you're not offended if we leave."

Florie waved her off. "No offense. I'll call you later." And just like that, Florie grabbed her walker and started inchin' towards the scoopers with an empty ice cream dish in one hand. There was a super-wide smile breaking out all over her face, like she was glad Renie had seen the light about the heat.

One thing you have to remember about Grandma Renie is that she has weighed a ton and a half her whole life. (Most of the weight came from ice cream served at ice cream festivals, I believe.) Gettin' her off her feet and into a car has always been a major production and it's somethin' I still hate.

"Be careful Granny," I said to her as she struggled to stand. "You're not the spring chicken you used to be."

At that she stood straight and grasped the bar of her walker. She glared at me first, then at the festival as General Patton would have at a German battlefield. Her words were meant to roast me. "Listen here, young man," she said, "I could run circles around you if I really wanted to. Fact is, I don't. Wouldn't want to show up good Talbott blood in front of all these people."

Just for fun I said, "All this talk of you runnin' circles sounds like mere bluff. Put up or shut up." And just to needle her further, I made several quick steps towards my car and motioned for her to follow like it was a race.

"I said I can't run!" she shouted before coughing twice into her hand. "Doctor says it would be none too good of me to go runnin' around like an idiot." She gestured towards her purse which was near her chair. "Could you please hand me my medicine? or must I get it myself!"

After fumblin' around in the world's biggest purse — it weighed ten tons — somehow I found her new blue pills with a French name stamped on them, they were the size of a guard dog's fang. My eyes got wide as saucers trying to imagine her swallowing just one of them — and she had to take two.

She said, "The reason I have to take such big pills is because of all you do to raise my blood pressure. All this worryin' is makin' me sick. You only visit once a month. Why, ever since your father and mother passed..."

I interrupted her. "Come on, Grandma, you're nearly a hundred. Your age is what's makin' you sick."

"I have you know, young man, that I intend on outlivin' my Aunt Birdie..."

"...who lived to be a hundred and two," I said, finishing her sentence for her. "I know, Grandma. You've told me that story a thousand times."

"And I intend on outlivin' Birdie, too!"

A glance at the festival crowd told me most of the City visitors had already vamoosed and that there was no one but town folk left to slobber at the ice cream trough. I was stayin' the night at Grandma's because I didn't like driving to The City after dark. Besides, stayin' with her meant I'd get to hear more stories about the way things were in oldtime Lake Moobegon. Couldn't miss that.

My Grandma Talbott is special. When me and my brothers were kids she used to sit by her ol' coal stove and spin stories of old days past, when life was better and altogether truly special. We used to wonder how she could keep so many memories straight for so long in that thick head of hers. She had a knack for makin' any story exciting. Aunt Louise figures she got that talent from her great uncle Squeezie whose chin I inherited and whose Bible I once scribbled on and ruined when I was 3.

Grannie can sit for hours — days, if need be — and tell how the Confederates burned down White Oak Bridge or how President McKinley got shot or what the soldiers looked like when they came home from World War I.

There's one story she doesn't tell that I wish she would. Most every Sunday when I was a kid, she and Grandpa would motor their red and white Ford Fairlane to Lake Moobegon Methodist Church to learn about Jesus. One reason Grandma liked church there was because they had those hand fans — you know, the kind that have the name of the local funeral home imprinted on the back? She used to tell me there was nothin' worse than sittin' on a sticky pew for two hours waitin' without hand fans for the minister to finish his sermon.

It wasn't until I was in my early 20s when Grandma started listening to all the radio preachers on WKRT-AM. She liked J. Vernon McGee, Billy Graham, Unshackled and Revival Time. Now I wished she had talked more about her faith in God. Most people in Lake Moobegon are like Grannie in that they don't usually share their faith with friends, even close friends, but rather save their special feelings for God in the privacy of prayer.

Though not perfect or even biblical, the Lake Moobegon method is better than most City folks handle their personal problems. I knowed one City man who to this day pays a psychiatrist with a wall full of degrees thousands of dollars a year just to sit and listen to him talk. Bein' a psychiatrist sure seems like a racket to me, especially since God listens for free.

FIVE

Cliff? I'm sorry, I forgot Cliff. He's been my best buddy for the better part of 30 years. We've known each other ever since the '60s when we played together at Lake Moobegon Elementary. His father owns the funeral home in town, you already know that, and his father has been teachin' Cliff the mortician business on weekends so Cliff can take over for him some day.

I grew up in Lake Moobegon but left for college in The City while Cliff stayed home and worked. We usually get together at the L.M.U.M.C.A.A.I.C.F. though Cliff couldn't make L.M.U.M.C.A.A.I.C.F. this year because he had to take his great aunt Flossie down to The City to get checked in at Mercy Hospital because of what she learned later was a painful bout of diverticulitis.

I could give you a detailed physical description of what Cliff looks like, boots to brains, so you'd have a decent mental picture, but that wouldn't mean a whole hill of beans today because all the stories in which I write about him have to do with years ago. He looks so much different now than when we were younger — so describin' him today might confuse you. For the sake of this book though, back then Cliff did look like all the other Lake Moobegon boys that wore flannel shirts, steel-toed work boots, and Wrangler's or Lee's if the Cyclone Store had them on sale. (To my knowledge, no one in Lake Moobegon has ever worn Levi's.)

Cliff and I got tight in Second Grade when we sat behind Nancy Druhot and tugged on her pig-tails until she told us to stop. We kept doing it because Nancy never ever turned us in to Mr. Peterson and because Cliff had a crush on her but he couldn't tell me that since she was a girl and boys that age aren't supposed to have crushes on girls anyway. Actually, I think she enjoyed the attention from Cliff because she always smiled a long time after he done it.

One day Cliff and I took ol' Nancy up on a bet and it was the dumbest thing we ever did. All three of us went down near the White Oak Creek Bridge to look for salamanders and it was there Nancy bet us that we wouldn't kiss the big oak tree for 30 seconds. At this age the last thing a boy wants to do is be around a girl, let alone taking one up on a bet as outrageous as kissin' a scraggly oak tree, but ol' Nancy held a strange power over Cliff especially. We not only kissed the tree but held that kiss longer than 30 seconds to show off.

We found out a week later that Cliff's parents had driven by and seen us at the exact moment our lips were pressed to tree bark. (Fifteen years after the tree incident Cliff married Nancy and they had three kids so it didn't turn out all bad.)

Cliff and I played ball in the summer at Lions Club Park on the east end of town. If you hit the ball real hard you could put it in the woods where the poison ivy was. I never could hit one in the woods but Cliff did a time or two. For some reason the Lions Club hardly ever cut their grass which meant the chiggers got real bad in leftfield. I know because I played leftfield.

It was out at Lions Club Park where Cliff had one of the funniest lookin' hits anybody in this county ever witnessed and people still talk about it to this day as if it were a legend. It's Cliff's claim to fame. If you count the number of people that swore they saw it you'd have a crowd; kind of like the people who swore they saw Babe Ruth point at the rightfield bleachers the time he hit the home run in Yankee Stadium.

In the late '60s during a big first round Little League tournament game, we were playing the Greenbush Bushers and Greenbush had this tall kid named Milt Somebody with big hands who could really hammer the ball. In fact he put two of them into the woods to give the Bushers a 4-1 lead goin' into the bottom half of the last inning.

Things didn't look good.

In our last at bat we somehow managed to get the bases loaded with two outs. That's when Cliff, only 10 then, walked to the plate. He was in a pressure-cooker situation if there has ever been one because he had to face Milt Somebody, also a pitcher, who was believed to be 12 and therefore too old for the league but we couldn't prove it. At the plate, Cliff shook like a leaf. His palms were sweatin' worse than a quart of Borden's ice cream floating in a jacuzzi. We thought his knees would buckle and they'd have to carry him off the field.

On the very first pitch this Milt Somebody throwed a most wicked curve ball, Cliff was ahead of it — it surprised him because he'd been ready for a fast ball he said later — and he swung right through it while the curve was only halfway to the plate. But wait! After swinging so early, Cliff had wound his bat around his body like a coiled-up snake and with a miracle of God the bat head, which was now behind him, found the curve as it finally crossed the inside corner and plunk, he hit it forward two feet. I had never seen anything like it in my life and I don't suppose I ever will again.

Cliff just stood there lookin' down at the baseball until Coach Cutlip yelled at him to run. So Cliff ran. The Bushers' catcher finally figured out what was goin' on, duh, and he picked up the ball and threw it towards first to end the game but it flew over the first baseman's head. It skittered into rightfield. Cliff kept runnin'. Their right fielder had trouble picking up the ball in the tall grass — thank you, Lions — and he winged it to the second baseman who scooped it up on one bounce and threw it over the third baseman's head and before you knew it ol' Cliff was stompin' across home plate with a grand slam run and we went nuts.

The scene of us mobbing home plate so flustered the Bushers that they argued extra hard with the umpire — Steve Gladden of Pickle's Cove — a good half-hour claiming that Cliff should have been ruled out because he had swung and missed, while we claimed there was nothin' in the rule book that said you couldn't swing twice. There was dead silence while Mr. Gladden checked the rule book. After five minutes of what looked like earnest prayer, Mr. Gladden scratched his head, shrugged, and said we had won. We went nuts again, this time even more so. It didn't matter that we went on to lose the next two games to Martin's Sink.

Miracles do happen.

Nowadays Cliff works at General Electric in The City makin' jet engine parts for fighter planes sold to Turkey or other places. He's been there better than 15 years and with God's help he'll get through the layoffs they're planning or at least until he goes full-time as a mortician when his dad retires. It takes a toll on a man to wake up at six in the morning, drive an hour in and then an hour back at night, but half the folks in Lake Moobegon do it because there's not much work in Hartan County save the Ford transmission plant down at Riplet.

"Cliff, how are you, you old rastus you?" I asked out Grandma Renie's side window not long ago.

I was on the inside this time while Cliff was outside.

"Dunkhead!" yelled Cliff, his souped-up Ford belchin' exhaust fumes. "When I heard you were back home, I raced over quick as I could. Just got back from Mercy Hospital. Aunt Flossie's in a terrible plight."

"What's wrong this time?

"Same ol' same ol'."

I paused a second to suck in clean air through my shirt sleeve. "Hope she gets better."

He bit his upper lip. "Me, too."

As an excuse to suck in more clean air, I leaned out the window towards a breeze and pounded on the hood of his stupid Ford. It was a diversionary tactic. "I'm surprised this old clunker still runs with that toy engine you got," I said. "I told you not to get a Ford but you wouldn't listen. You always was a hardhead."

"Now quit bad mouthin' Fords," he countered. "They're doin' a lot more right these days. It's not the same company it was in the '70s."

"I know, just like to needle you." He was right and I knowed it. "Hey, what you think of what old Johnny Lee did to Betsy at Fourth of July?"

Cliff shook his head in disgust. "Can you believe it?" he snorted. "I always said his parents had no business sendin' him to vocational school — why, that acetylene torch. Could've burned down the whole town, the clod."

"From what I hear from Brian and Alverna, Betsy wants him to buy her a new prom dress but Johnny Lee won't do it." I angled myself towards more clean wind, which was now flowing from the south. "Says she bought that dress for prom and he won't buy another unless she goes to another prom. Now if that ain't the most twisted logic I ever did hear. That was her senior prom and she won't have another."

Cliff said, "Johnny Lee always was kind of tight. Remember how he used to save his milk money? How any kid could go through six years of elementary school and just drink water from a fountain is beyond me."

I rolled my eyes. "Land yes, I remember that. He always was odd. But I guess we can't say anything bad against him because savin' like that did get him that nice home. I've even heard tell he's got a new fishin' boat with a nine-horsepower Evinrude."

Cliff reached over to crank his air conditioning up a notch, and to point the vent at his forehead. "Yep, yep," he agreed as the cool air flopped his hair around.

After a long pause, he changed the subject. "By the way, you hear my cousin Bobby Joe had a heart attack?"

"Oh, no. Not Bobby Joe! Where? When?"

Bobby Joe had put out twenty acres of tobacco by himself the previous year, which was a lot for a man with a full-time day job and four kids. Folks in Lake Moobegon plain work hard, takin' pride in what they do, makin' the most of their lot. I've known many a Lake Moobegon man who'll work eighteen hours a day at three jobs and do that at minimum wage rather than go on government assistance. It's their contribution to society.

After the awkward silence out of respect for Bobby Joe began fading away, I became curious about whether Cliff and Nancy would be at the big Eastern-Western football match-up. Cliff had missed it the year before because of strep throat. So I asked him.

He said, "You'd think I'd miss two years in a row? It would take a team of wild horses to keep me away, Lord willin'. I'm sick and tired of losin' to Western." For emphasis, he had to pound his dashboard. "Lord knows it's bad enough Western has uniforms. I just can't stand losin' to those wahoos." He pounded the dash two more times.

"It sure wasn't like that when we played. Coach would have killed us if we'd played Western the way they did last year. How do you fumble seven times and expect to win? If we lose this year the coach is gone."

After rubbing his left forearm — he was peeling off sunburned skin — Cliff got that look in his eye that he knew something I didn't. "Alverna down at the bank told me she knowed a women who overheard Brian the Head Teller say Coach Campbell is goin' to leave. Got offered a job down in the City at Woodward High School teachin' Social Studies makin' a lot more money than what we could pay him. Could be the best thing that's happened to Eastern football in years, I say."

"And the worst thing for Woodward," I added dryly.

"I just don't think we pass enough," Cliff said. "You can't expect to run the ball every first down and get away with it. Our offense is too predictable."

After rememberin' a whole slew of 20-yard punts and missed extra points from the last matchup, I had to add my two bits. "Half the time their punts get blocked and the other half it goes 20. You can't win if you give up field position like that. They should practice kicking more and that's the coach's fault."

"Well, you got a point."

"I knowed I got a point. I'm tellin' you what's wrong with the football team and anyone with half a brain can see it. It's the kickers."

"No, it's the offense."

"No, the kickers."

"Offense."

"Kicker..."

"Off.."

"Kick..."

Cliff always was a hardhead. Even when he knowed he was wrong he'd still hang in there with his wrong answer actin' like a fool long after he should've given up. He got his stubbornness from his mother Libby who was born a Fender. His dad seems to listen a lot more and that probably comes from having to deal with the live public all the time down at Lake Moobegon Rest-In-Peace Funeral Home.

I like Cliff a lot even though he's a hardhead. We have been friends through thick and thin and if he called today with a problem I'd help him in a minute, no matter the hour of day or night. I know he'd do the same for me. He's more a brother now that my real brothers are scattered across the country doin' their own thing.

SIX

By now you're probably wonderin' how I got nicknamed Dunkhead Danny. It has been embarrassing to talk about but it is common knowledge around town so I don't see how it would hurt tellin' you. Besides, it's better to hear the story from me rather than Cliff because he has a way of makin' it sound worse than it really was.

Way back in 1973 the Cincinnati Reds were in the National League playoffs for the third time in four years and we were expectin' them to win the pennant again, this time against the New York Mets before going on to the World Series where they rightfully belonged. Folks in Cincinnati were hungry for a World Championship. We'd lost two of the previous three: the first to Brooks Robinson and the Baltimore Orioles in '70 and the second to Gene Tenace and the Oakland Athletics in '72.

In 1973, as I watched the playoffs on TV, I couldn't believe my eyes. New York Mets fans were throwin' bottles, rocks and baseballs onto the field in an effort to hit our hero and saint #14 Peter Edward Rose — birthday April 14, bats both, throws right — for no good reason except he was The Great Peter Edward Rose. We couldn't swallow what their fans were doing. You'll never see folks actin' like that in Cincinnati.

Around Lake Moobegon, even today, #14 Peter Edward Rose is highly regarded despite all his alleged gambling problems that no intelligent person can honestly believe actually happened the way Major League Baseball said it did. I've been to Cincinnati Reds games and heard Johnny Bench booed, Joe Morgan booed, even Big Doggie Tony Perez, but never did I hear ol' Pete get booed by anyone. Pete is Cincinnati born and bred, gave 100 percent, and never slacked up, even as the Reds' manager. People overlook his faults because he hustled.

In one of those playoff games, all hell broke loose when Pete slid into second base spikes up while breakin' up a double play and that got the Mets' Bud Harrelson angry so Harrelson started a fistfight with Pete, which was like startin' a fight with Babe Ruth or Mordecai "Three Finger" Brown. The fight escalated and both teams went nuts and a brawl broke out. That was when the New York fans began throwin' bottles, rocks and baseballs. From that moment on we likened New York City to Sodom and Gomorrah and to this day you can't find anyone in Lake Moobegon who has a pleasant word to say about New York City. (Of course there wasn't a lot of goodwill for New York City even before the '73 playoffs but that's another story.)

"Don't take that from that runt."

"Hit him back."

"Get him, Pete."

"Come on, Pete."

"A left."

"Kick him."

Back then Cliff and I often made gentleman's bets in which the only thing either of us lost was pride or at worst a Snickers Bar or a vanilla cone with jimmies. However, every rule does have its exceptions, especially when your best friend thinks the Reds are goin' to lose to the Mets and you're shocked he's even thought of such an awful thing.

I blathered, "I betcha this fight gets us riled up enough to beat 'em."

Cliff shot back. "Betcha it won't. Betcha we lose in seven."

"Will too."

"Will not."

"Will."

"Won't."

Like I said earlier, Cliff always was a hardhead. Now he wanted the Reds to win just as much as I did and why he challenged me to a bet I still can't figure.

I stated my terms. "If the Reds win," I said with my tongue pressed hard to the inside of my mouth to keep from laughing at the sight of Cliff haulin' pancakes up to my bed in the morning, "you have to give me breakfast in bed for a week."

He replied immediately. "And if the Mets win you have to sit in the dunkin' booth on the Fourth of July the entire day."

I haven't told you about the dunking booth yet because I thought it might ruin this story but every July Fourth after the parade Mayor Cutlip's Little Leaguers set up a dunkin' booth in front of Ken's Barber Shoppe and charge a quarter for three throws in order to raise money to buy baseball equipment. Usually they get a pretty good response. The toughest part for them isn't raisin' money but in gettin' people to sit on that stupid platform all day long waitin' for folks to hit the target and then you're all wet.

Cliff could have been a real sportsman and kept the bet to himself but as soon as the Mets won he went around blabbin' to the whole town about how he'd won. Just like him to do that. And as if that wasn't enough, next thing I hear he was down at Mayor Cutlip's office and after that the next thing I knowed the Mayor's Little Leaguers were takin' dunkin' booth advance ticket sales — ADVANCE ticket sales — and by Memorial Day they had sold 103. From then on I knowed I was in for a rough go.

On July Fourth after the parade, Cliff eased me out onto the platform that hovered over the water tank and it was at that moment I realized how desperate a situation I was in. Glarin' at me with lustful eyes was Mayor Cutlip's Little Leaguers dressed up in crisp Dairy Whip uniforms. (They had never before dressed up for the dunkin' booth.) Some of them were playin' catch with the advance ticket people to warm them up. Eighteen kids, all with catcher's mitts and spikes, all loaded for bear.

They had gone around town that morning and put up signs with my picture on them. I don't know how they got my picture but it wasn't a bad one, my Four-square School Champion photo from elementary school with the word "WANTED" plastered over top like I was some Post Office felon from Sing Sing.

The one thing I try not to remember about that day was droppin' off that platform time after time after time after time after time until I felt like a wet O-Cello sponge. At first it felt nice because of the heat but it got real old fast. My skin shriveled up like I was some huge white raisin.

Cliff said I got dunked 197 times but I lost count after 15, maybe it was 33, I can't remember which. At times they were lined up 25 deep.

To my shock, when it got dark and I was ready to leave, Mayor Cutlip rumbled his metallic green Ford LTD station wagon right up to the platform and with his left foot he clicked on the high beams. Those Little Leaguers kept throwin' at me in the dark for two more hours all the way through midnight. I got soaked. I tried to be a good sport about it, and laugh, but when you get dunked 197 times it gets to you a little.

The *News Democrat* reporter wrote about my losin' the bet and the dunking. I did get my picture on the front page though, my one moment in the sun. Such publicity led to me bein' called Dunkhead Danny for all eternity and then some.

Needless to say that was the last time I bet on anything. Too bad Peter Edward Rose couldn't have learned the same lesson or else today he would be sittin' in Baseball's Hall of Fame at Cooperstown, New York, where he rightfully belongs alongside Shoeless Joe Jackson, Mordecai "Three Finger" Brown and Johnny Bench.

The only locals that don't call me Dunkhead are Grandma Renie, Uncle Johnny, and some old folks from Johnny's generation who still feel sorry for me.

SEVEN

Cliff and I compete in everything. Doesn't matter what it is: runnin', throwin', spittin', tree climbin'. We've even competed over who could hit Brian the Head Teller's oak tree the most times with sweet gum balls. Usually all our competition is done in a gentlemanly manner because we're friends, but there was one time in our past when we didn't compete at all friendly-like and I guess that time needs explainin'.

About a month after Cliff's grand slam and when he was still the talk of the Greater Lake Moobegon area, me and him got to jabberin' one day about who the best athlete was between us. I was more than content to say we were equals, which we had always been, but he had to disagree. It was that grand slam of his that made him better, he said. His pride was puffed up bigger than a bullfrog's throat and his attitude downright arrogant.

He said he was the best athlete between us and all I need do was look at what he had done and that he was the greatest. WHAT HAD HE DONE? HE WASN'T THE GREATEST! I told him his "hit" wasn't official because of the errors but he wouldn't hear nothing of it. He said cream always rose to the top, which was the kind of talk that really got my blood boilin'. Our friendship had always been based on the premise that we were equals.

"So you think you're pretty hot stuff, don't you?" I said.

He held his chin high, smirked. "Like I said, cream always rises to the top."

"Why, you sound conceited."

"I am not conceited," he said, his chest puffin' out like Tarzan's. "I'm just tellin' the truth. Fact is, I'm destined for glory, you aren't and there's no two ways about it. With some people events fall into place and with others they don't." Then he stuck an index finger in my face. "Take you, for instance, Talbott. Now if you'd a gotten a hit before me that day against the Bushers, I wouldn't a had to hit that grand slam. *You* could've been the hero and had braggin' rights."

I had to rub my ears because I couldn't believe what I had just heard. "Excuse me? My hit was a lot better than yours. It was a liner, not a dumb dribbler out in front of the plate that took two swings to hit. I just happened to hit mine hard at the leftfielder."

"But the truth of the matter is you made an out, didn't you? And remember last year when you dropped that ball against Pickle's Cove? You could have been the hero of that game, too."

That was below the belt. "Hey, wait a dag burn minute here!"

Cliff went on. "Well, you could have won that one. Ain't that right?"

"You couldn't have caught that ball. Why, I was divin'..."

52

"But you didn't catch it, did you?"

He was really making me angry, so I snarled at him real hard. "So what you tryin' to say? That you're the best athlete between us? Is that it? You're best?"

He replied with an air of conceit. "No, I'm just sayin' I know I'm the best. Some people are destined for glory and others like you aren't."

"Not true."

"True."

"Not true."

"True."

"There is only one way to resolve this, Cliff. I'm challenging you to a fight." I knew he wouldn't back down from a fight because he couldn't back down. He had to fight me because if he didn't I'd call him scaredy chicken and there was nothin' worse in Lake Moobegon than being called scaredy chicken. A long pause later he swallowed hard. "Okay," he said, "a fight it is, at the feed mill, tomorrow after school."

And have it be like Cliff to tell the whole town. There was a good 50 folks at the mill, mostly classmates, and two adults, Old Ben Dunn and Elmer Wardlaw. I'd never seen such a crowd. My guess was Cliff figured I wouldn't fight him in front of a crowd but he was wrong if that was his strategy. This time I was goin' to teach him a lesson he'd never forget.

"Guns or knives?"

His jaw dropped a foot. "What you mean, guns or knives?"

This was my shining moment in Lake Moobegon folklore, yes, even bigger than being Dunkhead Danny on July Fourth, and what a moment it would be. (Andy Warhol said everyone has 15 minutes of fame. I had mine twice.) In full view of all including Nancy, Cliff's future wife, I pulled out a velvet case from under my Cincinnati Bengals sweater that had Virgil Carter's #12 on it. I undid the latch and lifted the lid to reveal my Uncle Johnny's ancient duelin' pistols and two army knives I had borrowed from my father who had been in Korea. I'd shined the pistols the night before so they would gleam extra special in the sunlight and the knives were so sharp they glistened like ice.

Cliff looked scaredy chicken and everybody knowed he was scaredy chicken.

For added effect I let loose a monster load of slobber so it would dribble off my mouth in a huge vein all the way to the ground. I pointed at him and screamed bloody murder like a madman. "YOU SCAREDY CHICKEN?" I began mussing my hair up, and gave him my best hairy eyeball.

It was just an act of course and a pretty convincing one at that because Cliff's Adam's apple was startin' to bob up and down like it always did when he was afraid during monster movies. "I am not scaredy chicken," he said, his voice cracking. "Fact is, I just don't see a need for knives. I'd slice you up with one." His Adam's apple was bobbin' up and down even faster now, like a piston in first gear.

I went for the jugular. "Ha! Real men use guns and knives while babies use fists. So what's it going to be, Clifford LaMar Fender? I've about had enough of that uppity mouth of yours. Mark my words, this will end up with one of us dead and it ain't going to be me. Your own father is going to have to come pick you up in a plastic bag."

(People told me later that I had a serious look in my eyes and my neck veins popped and the way I had said "dead" would have scared anyone, even the Green Hornet or Batman. In fact, my performance was so good Eastern High School's drama teacher, who witnessed it all, later offered me the starring role in her drama club's production of "The Three Little Bears." I was to play the Big Bad Wolf but my mom made me turn the part down because of a dentist appointment, she said, but I think it was because she didn't want me to hurt Cliff's feelings any further.)

"I mean it, Cliff. Either you or me is going to die."

He was thinking. After what seemed like an eternity — his brain was whirring in thought — he began slowly slinking away, his head down, moving towards humiliation and the Cyclone Store. It was a sad sight. He had been beat bad because I had called his bluff by bluffing him. As he slinked off he kicked rocks.

He walked away but then a block down the road he turned and started runnin' arms flailing right back at me. The crowd cheered him. He said he wanted a wrestlin' match instead of the guns and knives. The crowd booed him. (I wouldn't have done the guns or knives thing even if you'd paid me $2,000,000.) Cliff pounded his chest and said wrestlin' was a man's sport. The crowd and I weren't buyin' it. We all knew he was trying to save face. From that moment on everybody knew Cliff Fender was at heart a scaredy chicken.

I agreed to the wrestlin' match because I felt sorry for him. We wrestled in the feed mill dust for three rounds and we each won one and tied one. We were dirtier than pigs. After that afternoon Cliff never got uppity again and I never again tried takin' him down a notch. Friends should leave the humbling business to God.

EIGHT

Uncle Johnny Talbott is a character and a half. He's my father's brother and we just love him to pieces especially at Christmas when he's the life of the party. I have a love/hate relationship with him. I love to have him around because he's so much fun but hate it when he grabs onto your knee and tickles it until you nearly die laughin'. Uncle Johnny owns a grocery store in Martin's Sink along the Greenbush Road. He does a good business because he doesn't have competition.

The only big store around is Superette Food King up at Fayettesburg, which is a good 7,000 sq. ft., but their shopping cart wheels don't work right. They wiggle to the side and make black marks that need constant scrubbing.

Uncle Johnny is real particular about his store's cleanliness, and he tries to mold that same particularness into his dozen employees. No black marks on his floor. He'd love to own a grocery store closer to Lake Moobegon but the Fender brothers have Lake Moobegon all sewed up and there's room enough for only one grocery in that town.

I worked for Uncle Johnny a few summers in the '70s and that's how I learned the grocery business and that's how I got the good job I have now as a grocery salesman for a mega-company you'd instantly know by its recognizable name. Johnny had me doin' everything: I filled milk, condensed eggs, wrapped lettuce, even reset the Kool-Aid and Country Time Lemonade section twice.

Produce is the best job in the world because you deal with folks on a personal basis, and it's not rushed. Only problem is you don't do beans in the summer because of competition from nearby roadstands and people's gardens. Believe it or not, Johnny's biggest competition in the summer comes from his own mother, Grandma Renie, who sells strawberries roadside. Recently he's been tryin' to get her to sell strawberries to him so he can resell them at the grocery.

He says he wants her strawberries off the market but she won't take them off.

"This is America," she says, "and I'm free to sell whatever I want, whenever I want, and to whoever I want." Maybe it's just me, but I don't think she cares about the money she makes. She enjoys needling her son.

Which reminds me of a story. One Saturday evening back when I worked for Uncle Johnny, a few minutes away from closin' up the grocery — Uncle Johnny closed every Sunday — Barbara Ann the Aisle #2 Stocker noticed something strange and I noticed him, too. He was a young man with hippie red hair, farmer overalls, a man we'd never seen before, who was stuffin' T-bones down his pants at the meat counter like they were goin' out of style. I just didn't see how he expected us not to notice him because what he was doin' was plainer than a pig in a sheep pen.

He tried waddlin' up Aisle #1 and out the "in" door but we had warned Uncle Johnny so he was there lookin' real stern when he asked the young man what he was doin' waddlin' out the door with pants full of T-bones. The shoplifter had the gall to say "What meat?" and to tell Uncle Johnny to "get out of my way."

"Young man, do you know what's goin' to happen to you if you leave this here store with those T-bones tucked down your pants?"

"First off mister, I don't have no T-bones tucked down my pants, and second off, you're an ol' fart and you can't catch me anyway."

"Try me."

In my opinion that man was signing his own death warrant by calling Uncle Johnny ol' fart because it was somethin' you just didn't say to older folk.

The instant the shoplifter waddled out the electric door, Uncle Johnny instructed Melba The Head Cashier to telephone the Ohio State Trooper. She reached for the phone. Then with the shoplifter 20 yards ahead and pullin' away, Uncle Johnny tore off after him like an angry dog and in my whole life I had never seen the likes of what would happen next.

Normally that young man would outrun Johnny any day of the week — anybody could outrun Uncle Johnny, land sakes, even a pregnant dachsund or a four-toed sloth. You have to remember that this shoplifter was weighed down with T-bones and couldn't move his legs much or else he'd lose the meat. While he was runnin' across the field next to the grocery the young man turned to yell at Johnny. "You can't catch me ol' man so there's no use tryin'."

"I'm gonna catch you if it's the last thing I do."

Off they went across the field, down U.S. 68 towards New Hope, over the B&O railroad tracks, across Ditterlein's corn field, around Vance's apple orchard. The shoplifter doubled back, crossed the B&O again and zipped towards Martin's Sink Town Hall. Uncle Johnny was right behind the whole time but it seemed like he was almost dyin' of a heart attack. I guess his pride wouldn't let him stop. (I know all this because I was right behind them. I was tryin' to catch up fast but this stupid price gun kept bangin' against my hip and the tape kept unraveling.)

"Come on ol' man," the shoplifter said between spare breaths, "why don't you just quit?"

"I'm gonna catch you, you young whippersnapper."

Whippersnapper is an awfully long word to say when you've been runnin' for the better part of a mile but the State Trooper swore he heard Johnny say it and I think I did, too.

The shoplifter spied the State Trooper when he turned the corner onto U.S. 68 and the State Trooper smiled right back while restin' in his police cruiser, smokin' a Pall Mall. Melba's call had gotten through. Before the State Trooper could get out to make an arrest, Uncle Johnny snuck up and tackled the shoplifter. They wrestled in the pea rock gravel until Johnny pinned him. Most of the meat fell out of the shoplifter's pants and T-bone blood ran over both their clothes and mixed in with the gravel and made them look bloody.

"You're hurtin' my knee."

"I'm not lettin' you up until you say you're sorry."

The shoplifter grunted. "Of-fi-cer, make this ol' fart stop."

The shoplifter didn't know Uncle Johnny and the State Trooper were horseshoe pitchin' buddies. After the shoplifter said "ol' fart" the State Trooper lit another Pall Mall. He let Uncle Johnny have his way for five more minutes while the shoplifter squirmed in the T-bone blood and gravel.

"Let go!" he whined. "Officer, help!"

Uncle Johnny did release him. When he did the shoplifter crumpled in a ball, just layin' there wailin' like a baby that needed changing. Pitiful sight.

"Should I press charges?" Uncle Johnny asked the State Trooper.

The State Trooper shrugged his shoulders, blew a smoke ring.

Uncle Johnny glared down at the shoplifter. "I'll make a deal with you. If you promise to work for me for a week at half pay, I won't press charges. That'll take care of your debt for the meat and I'll be satisfied."

The shoplifter yelled, "What? You crazy? I ain't workin' for you."

Uncle Johnny grimaced. "I guess you'll have to spend a right long time in jail then. Ain't that right Mr. State Trooper?"

The State Trooper blew more smoke out, this time in a short burst. "Mr. Thief, you could be lookin' at a long stay in the city hoosegow, especially since we caught you with the evidence. T-bone blood don't lie. Kind of hot in jail this time of year, hundred, hundred twenty maybe on a day like today. Of course, the judge may let you off the hook but given he's this man's cousin," he said, pointing his lit cigarette at Uncle Johnny, "it don't look too good for you now, does it?"

The shoplifter gulped. "Uh, oh."

(The State Trooper wasn't being totally truthful. Judge Norman Vincent Beale wasn't Uncle Johnny's real cousin but a second cousin by marriage.)

"What you goin' to make me do at that grocery store of yours? I'm not workin' for you if I got to scrub floors all day."

Uncle Johnny said, "What you'll be doin' is my business, not yours. If you work for me you'll do exactly what you're told. Is that understood?"

He shrugged his shoulders, began standing up. "Show me the way ol' man."

"First thing we get straight: My name's Johnny Talbott; Mr. Talbott to you. It's not ol' man. Second, if you get the idea you can run off before your week's out then I give you my word I'll track you down, tackle you like I did here, and next time my cousin will throw the book at you. You hear me?"

"Yes, sir."

His name was Billy Hanselmann. He'd run away from his folks but Uncle Johnny couldn't send him back because they didn't want any part of him. They said he was a troublemaker. According to his own account, Billy had been livin' at the deserted McCoy place and had gotten food by beggin' and stealin'.

Believe it or not Billy turned out to be a right nice worker and by week's end Uncle Johnny asked him to stay on. Seemed crazy at the time but to this day Billy's a loyal employee. Now he runs the meat department. He's Head Meat Cutter.

Later Billy told us he was on the Busher team that lost to Cliff's grand slam. It had been the toughest defeat of his entire baseball career, he said. In fact, he was the rightfielder who picked up his catcher's bad throw and threw it on one bounce to the second baseman who threw it over the third baseman's head. Small world, ain't it?

NINE

Uncle Johnny has been known as the most progressive businessman in Hartan County ever since Elmer Stone, the Mercury Marketing Maniac, died in 1969. Besides givin' Billy that second chance he has also been the main force behind Martin's Sink "One Cent Sidewalk Sale." The town's businesses set the first Saturday in December aside for it. A few folks wait for the "One Cent Sidewalk Sale" to do the bulk of their Christmas shopping but most go because it's the right thing to do. Johnny has been recognized by most Hartan Countians as a marketing genius because of it. I think they're right, but of course I'm partial.

The One Cent Sidewalk Sale has been such a success the businessmen in Lake Moobegon are jealous of Martin's Sink's and now they want their own. In fact, Mayor Cutlip was quoted in the *News Democrat* as saying "there definitely will be a Lake Moobegon One Cent Sale next year," but there is still a debate over timing. Most Lake Moobegon business owners want it the week before Martin's Sink's, which would make it the first of December, but Mayor Cutlip wants it July Fourth to tie in with the parade, the dunkin' booth and also because July is peak time for the Dairy Whip. Just imagine all the banana boats he'd sell. Nobody buys banana boats in December.

There has been a rivalry between Lake Moobegon and Martin's Sink since the early 1900s when both towns vied for the feed mill — at least that is what Grandma Renie told me. Lake Moobegon won the bidding war by selling railroad land to the Cutlips for a dollar and givin' the feed mill a 20-year exemption on taxes. Martin's Sink couldn't match that because their town didn't own land along the railroad. Some older Martin's Sinkers are still bitter about the whole thing.

Mayor Cutlip's grandfather, Elias Cutlip VI, accepted Lake Moobegon's offer and moved his mill by rail down from Ashtabula. The town still rewards the Cutlips every four years by choosing a Cutlip as mayor. Bein' mayor doesn't pay beans, just a thousand, but the title's nice and you can double park all you want. The Cutlips have a system of rotating the office among themselves and I do believe every adult Cutlip has served at least once.

(There was talk — now whether it was true or not, I don't know — of the Cutlips runnin' their dog for mayor, a collie-lab, Prissy, but it created such a stink that some folks were plannin' on runnin' against the canine if it ever came to that.)

Uncle Johnny started the One Cent Sidewalk Sale thing five years ago because Martin's Sink was losin' business when folks began drivin' into The City to do their Christmas shopping. To stop the retail bleeding loss the town's businesses agreed to set up shop in front of their stores the first of December to get rid of slow movers. The gimmick was to buy one item at regular price and get a second for one cent.

Everything worked fine until two years ago when the town had an early winter and the temperature hit ten degrees for a high. No one showed up because of the cold. To rescue his baby Uncle Johnny moved all the businessmen down to Martin's Sink Lion's Club Hall where there was kerosene heat and free parking. In fact, it worked out so well they did it again the next year.

When Uncle Johnny takes his damaged grocery goods down the town folk seem grateful because they know there's nothin' wrong with the product. They snatch it up like it's Bumble Bee Tuna or Wheaties. Last year Johnny did $978 worth of business in four hours and could have done more had he more damaged product. He even sold two cases of the Chock Full O'Nuts Coffee that had been tucked underneath his back door receiver's desk gathering dust for the better part of two years. Nobody around here had even tried Chock Full O'Nuts before because they thought it was a mixture of coffee and Spanish peanuts. I think someone from Chock Full O'Nuts needs to get down here and explain exactly what's in that coffee.

The big surprise of last year's One Cent Sale came when Cliff's father, the mortician, bought a case of damaged STP Gas Treatment from Randy's Auto Center. We still wonder what he uses it for. Cliff Jr. claims they don't use it in the hearse.

Every year I make the trip in from The City. Three years ago, when they were havin' it outside, I bought two winter coats with hoods and zippers that worked from Martin's Sink General Store. I wrapped them both up and gave them to Cliff and Nancy as "his and hers" winter coats. They like romantic stuff like that.

"You mean to tell me that if I buy one can opener you're gonna sell me another one for one cent?" I asked Otto Barnes who owned Martin's Sink General Store.

He ran his hands through silvery hair. "That's right, young man."

I scratched my head. "Why do I need two can openers?"

"Well?" he said as he flattened his palm towards me, "just listen a minute. If you break one can opener, you always got a spare. So havin' an extra one gives you peace of mind. Second, if you got an extra one, you always got the option of takin' that one on vacation. That way you won't have to buy another at full price on your vacation. And if a neighbor stops by askin' for a can opener, you can help them without givin' up your only one. So's you see, there are lots of reasons to buy a second can opener."

"I never thought of it like that. Sign me up and give me your best two. I know a good deal when I see it."

Jake the Used Car Dealer unloads his clunkers at the One Cent Sale. His lot sits on the Greenbush Road near Uncle Johnny's Supermarket. Not too many people like or trust him but the closest dealer besides him is 20 miles south. I think everyone tolerates him because they have to.

The first year of the sale Brian Shaw bought one car for himself and another for his son — that was one at full price, the second for a cent. It was front page news for the *News Democrat* so they sent a reporter to interview Brian. Seemed no one had ever bought two cars at once in Hartan County.

"What's it like to be the first man in Hartan County to buy two cars at once?"

Brian shrugged his shoulders. "Sir, I don't feel any different."

The newspaperman licked his pencil, scribbled a few notes. "You happy with Jake's deal?"

"Yep. Don't know about Milo, though. He got the other. I guess he's got to drive it and see what happens. You never know with Jake."

"You be comin' back next year?"

"Depends on whether the sale conflicts with opening week at the tobacco auction in Riplet. If it doesn't, I'm here."

Brian's son, Milo — his car did break down after a week but he couldn't complain given the price. He ended up sellin' it for parts and used the $200 as a down payment on a truck he would later buy in Riplet. Got a right nice Chevy pick-up for less than a thousand, and he had enough extra to add a camper top and dangle dice from the rearview.

Brian drives his car to this day. It's an '89 Ford Taurus with tinted glass, mud flaps, bronze baby shoes hangin' from the rearview and a liquid-filled dashboard compass that points mostly northeast.

Ellis Shaw's real estate agency — if you haven't figured it out already, Ellis Shaw is Brian Shaw's father and Milo's grandfather — he joined the marketing fray last year and offered a One Cent Sale on Martin's Sink town lots he bought a few years back at Jeb Wardlaw's estate sale. Didn't work out as they expected because everyone in Martin's Sink already had a lot and didn't need another, let alone two. I suppose the only folks buyin' those lots will be City folk looking for a second home. They could sit a while.

Now that it's true and tested, I suspect Uncle Johnny's One Cent Sale idea will spread like wildfire to retail stores in Cincinnati or Maysville, Kentucky. Pretty soon you'll be hearin' of all kinds of items sold that way — boats, coats, swimming pools, airplanes, tractors, tobacco barns, church buildings. Just stands to reason, if you got a good idea stick with it.

TEN

Church rivalry. No, not church revival, but church r-i-v-a-l-r-y.

I spent an awful lot of time as a youth at Lake Moobegon Church of Christ and got to know the people there. The church was located smack dab in the middle of town on a lot across from Ken's Barber Shoppe near the four-way stop. The pastor, a youthful man, Pete Cordray, grew the church from 80 to the 175 they now have. Back when I was there they were higher than 125 only once, and that was for Elmer and Ireta Wardlaw's Gospel duet on Sunday night and the very lively punch and cookie reception that followed.

Things changed for the better when Rev. Pete came to town fresh from a Cincinnati seminary on fire for God. He had ideas about church growth, ministries to ol' folk, daycare, door-to-door evangelism. Most of us were excited because he was excited, we truly felt happy for him, but deep-down we wondered what the big fuss was all about because we couldn't see challengin' the Baptists' vise-grip on local church attendance.

The Baptists had 300 and were lookin' to build an education wing and a new parsonage. We were just a town church with a bumper crop of old folk, a new shingle roof and a paid-off mortgage.

Pete didn't want to steal sheep but some Baptists did church-hop when they heard all he was doing. That's when Shorty McGuire found out more than a few Baptists had seen Pete as a threat. So before they and even we realized it, we had a right-nice church rivalry on our hands.

First thing, Rev. Pete asked the elders for money to buy a yellow church bus. They decided to humor him — after all, they had the rainy day money that had never been touched and a deacon, Shorty McGuire, who was a certified Ford and AMC mechanic — so they voted to give the bus thing a try. Quite a few of us, myself included, questioned the smarts of buyin' a church bus when nearly all of us lived within walkin' distance of the church.

"What you think of the new preacher?"

"Like his sermons and all, but..."

"But what?"

"But...but!"

"Come on, out with it."

"Well, I just think ol' Pete might be goin' overboard with this bus thing."

"You're not the only one that thinks that way."

"What do you think?"

"I agree he might be overdoin' it, if you know what I mean."

"Uh-huh."

"What we need a bus for anyway? Most everybody walks to church."

"'Suspect it will be real nice takin' the team to softball games in a big bus. That's what the Baptists do with theirs."

"Suppose we could always use it to pick up the widows."

"But don't all the widows live in town?"

"Yep."

"Aren't you worried about us spendin' all that money buyin' a bus and then havin' no use for it?"

"Naw. I figure if we end up not usin' it the Baptists'll buy it from us. They could use another one anyway."

That's what everyone figured since Shorty McGuire was the Baptist preacher's mechanic, they got along well, and Shorty told us he probably could talk the pastor into buyin' it if need be. But that never happened. In fact, after two months of using the bus we were beginnin' to liken Pete to geniushood. You know what he did? He went door-to-door out on the farms to invite people to church and he used the bus to pick them up — an idea I thought was nigh brilliant. Before long average attendance was up 30 because of the bus people and that didn't even count the church hoppers.

The biggest benefit we got from it all was one we hadn't planned on. We got a burly lookin' character who eventually tipped the spiritual balance of power in the Lake Moobegon church community permanently in our favor. His name was Andy Holbrook. Yes, THE Andy Holbrook.

Big Andy, as he was called, was a legend in Hartan County Sports History by the time we got him. He was the first inductee into the Hartan County Athletic Hall of Fame — a treasured shrine, located near the AT&T pay phone at the Riplet Fire Hall — and the first person folks would mention when outsiders asked if there had ever been a famous person from Hartan County. Andy was it.

My dad once showed me an old 8mm film of him hittin' a baseball in high school and boy could he hit. He put it into a cow pasture once and I marked off the spot where Dad said it landed and it was 423 feet. Andy went as far as Triple A in the San Francisco Giants farm system and would have gone on to the majors had it not been for gettin' hit in the left eye by a fastball one foggy night in Spokane. Ruined a great baseball career.

When we got him he was in his mid-40s and in great shape from balin' hay and tossin' manure on the dairy farm he'd bought with his pro baseball signin' bonus. Apparently, Rev. Pete had stopped by to explain the Gospel and Andy was so touched that Jesus loved him enough to die for his sins that he pledged to attend church every Sunday from that day forward. When he did come he sat in the front row where no one had sat previously.

He couldn't have come at a better time. Up until then the First Baptist Church had owned church softball in Hartan County. They had 100 grown men to draw on and every spring their coach would skim the cream with tryouts the first two weeks of April. Tryouts! Tryouts for a church softball team! We were lucky to get ten to fill out a lineup card let alone have tryouts and cuts. They even had a player named Bobby Nicholson who could hold five baseballs in his hand while whistlin' "He's got the whole world in His hands."

Something miraculous happened the day Big Andy decided to join our Church of Christ softball team. All of a sudden we had a flood of men, men we hadn't seen before, all showin' up at church and beggin' Pastor Pete to let them play with Andy. Reverend Pete was lovin' it because he had a team rule that said if you didn't attend church on Sunday you couldn't play. That meant all these men flockin' to play were also going to get a Sunday sermon.

That first summer with Big Andy was the greatest sports summer of my life, bar none, even greater than the summer of Cliff's famous home run that people still talk about from time to time. I was 18 and feelin' almost growed up and big enough to finally hit the ball as far as a regular man. Eighteen games we played that summer but none was better than that first game against the Baptists. It was softball perfection.

Like I said, up until then the Baptists thought they walked on water. In the 14-year history of the Hartan County Church Softball League the Baptists had won the title 13 times. The one year they didn't win was when their bus broke down on the way to the 1967 Championship Game which they had to forfeit because they arrived two minutes after the legal forfeiture time. We still have the trophy. That was when I was knee-high to a duck and I don't remember much except we won. The Baptists blamed it on Shorty McGuire and indirectly he was to blame because it was his alternator that broke down.

But this year was different. I can just imagine the conversation they had when we pulled up in our church bus before the game.

Bobby Nicholson pointed at us and said, "Look, Jerry, here comes the Church of Christ in their new bus. Don't know why they even bother to show."

Jerry laughed. "Ha-ha. What a bunch of losers."

"Heard tell they got a much improved team, though. Rumor is they got Andy Holbrook." (Andy's name was always whispered the same way you'd whisper Babe Ruth or Pete Rose.)

"They still have to field nine. I don't care how good he is, one man can't beat us."

Bobby scratched his temple as we piled off the bus. "Hey, isn't that Billy Fender? Since when did he start church there? He's a good ball player."

Jerry planed his hand over the bill of his cap. "That's Mayor Cutlip's son, too. What's he doin' here? Didn't he play for the University of Dayton?"

We were stacked and they knew it. Felt right nice gettin' off that bus. You could see them lookin' over at us, watchin' us flex and stretch our muscles, looking at how fast we could sprint, seein' if we were afraid. We had on blue windbreakers with "MSCC" printed on the back in bright yellow letters. The windbreakers were Andy Holbrook's idea because he wanted us to look and feel like winners.

Since they were home team, we batted first. First man up was Billy Fender and BAM he got a hit, second man up was Cutlip's son and BAM he got a hit, third man up was Reverend Pete and he walked. Then Andy Holbrook stepped to the plate with the bases loaded and you could have heard a pin drop.

In the previous 14 years the Baptists had lost only two games. (One was by forfeit to us and we still can't figure out how the Methodists beat them straight up the one time.) By now we all had this feeling like we were in the midst of sports history in the making. And indeed we were. We knew Andy was goin' to hit the ball, we just didn't know where.

Andy hit it all right, on the first pitch and I can still see it now as it rises over the leftfielder's head, over the hickory trees, over the meadow, and, well, that's the kind of hit legends are made of. It was over 360 feet which is a whole lot for a red-dot softball. We went nuts. Greatest moment in Hartan County sports history. Babe Ruth couldn't have hit one that far.

You remember those ol' film clips of Babe Ruth, and the way he used to round first base real wide? I am tellin' you no lie but Andy looked exactly like ol' Babe when he rounded the bag with his belly jigglin' like Jell-O. Everybody was jumpin' up and down crazy-like. Cliff pulled a leg muscle because he was jumpin' up and down so much and I lost all sensibilities and tripped over the bat rack and fell down in a pile of Louisville Sluggers. It didn't matter though. Nothing mattered.

We crushed them 22-12 and haven't lost to them or anyone else since. The whole softball thing has brought on a revival among the men at church who play. Out of all the newcomers, five now have a new heart for God. Billy Fender became a deacon; Andy Holbrook, an elder.

The Baptists were so rattled by the incident that they started a full-blown membership drive — my guess, partly to win some of their pride back. They bought a second bus and up shot their attendence with it. Ours shot up, too. Seemed like both churches shot up and I guess God was pleased by it all. He certainly works in mysterious ways.

ELEVEN

Bagneesh. Just Bagneesh. We never knew his last name. In fact, he said we couldn't pronounce it even if we knew it so he never bothered to teach us. He arrived in late '73 and forever changed my outlook on life and opened up my horizons to far away places. I attribute my decision to go to college on the influence he had on my life. I'm thankful for that.

Mayor Cutlip said all along he'd wanted to sponsor an exchange student from a faraway land because he thought it would bring media attention to our area and therefore enhance Lake Moobegon's status as the trendsetters of Hartan County.

But we knew better. We figured he wanted to sponsor an exchange student to make his son, Tommy, the talk of the town. Tommy was always buggin' his dad to do showy things because he wanted to be popular with the girls and to win the student council president election as a junior, which he didn't. Then again it would be only a matter of time before Martin's Sink got the idea of bringing in a foreign exchange student, so maybe the Mayor felt like he had to do it for that.

For whatever reason, he signed up with an exchange service and requested someone from a foreign land: Indiana.

Bagneesh came on a sunny day two weeks before school was to start, just a week after L.M.U.M.C.A.A.I.C.F. Mayor Cutlip did the expected and borrowed the Marching Highlander Band and Drill Team from Western High School for the event.

(It was embarrassing to admit but Eastern has never had a band or drill team because it can't afford uniforms. Western didn't seem to mind playing for Eastern on occasion because they said it gave them a place to practice.)

The moment Bagneesh's bus screeched to a stop — he came in on the Greyhound that travels Cincinnati to West Virginia — the Western band began a real nice rendition of B.J. Thomas' hit song "Raindrops Keep Fallin' on My Head." The Cutlips had decorated Main Street with red and white balloons because they figured their exchange student would take kindly to Indiana Hoosier colors.

The sky was blue. I had goose pimples. I felt proud for my hometown because it would soon be home to the first-ever foreign exchange student in Hartan County history. In fact, Mayor Cutlip was so proud he ended up puttin' that very slogan on a glossy welcome sign out on the Old Cincinnati Road entrance to town. "Home of First-Ever Foreign Exchange Student in Hartan County."

(We wanted another sign on the Buford Road entrance but there wasn't enough money in the budget. Since the Mayor lived on Old Cincinnati Road guess where the sign went? The next year there was further talk of adding a Buford Road sign, but there wasn't enough signatures to force it onto the November ballot as a bond issue and since then folks have let the issue die.)

Bagneesh stepped off the bus into dead silence. The only one who made a noise was Western's lone tuba player and that was because he couldn't see what was happenin' since his tuba was too big.

I saw a scrawny lookin' kid not much older than 14 with the darkest skin I had ever seen. A towel was wrapped around his head. He was wearing an all-black suit in the middle of summer. The way he was dressed I wondered what city in Indiana he could be from.

Mayor Cutlip walked up to him — exhaust fumes from the bus were still churning the air around them both — and seemed to study him careful-like from head to toe. In fact, everybody studied him carefully from head to toe like he was some frog in a jar. I think the black suit really startled us. As the bus roared off towards West Virginia we just continued studying him in silence like he was some frog in a jar.

He broke the silence. "Are you Meester Cutlip?" he asked.

"I am *MAYOR* Cutlip!" The Mayor said, his chest puffed out as if he were President of the United States or something. "I'm MAYOR of Lake Moobegon! And who are you?"

He squeaked. "I am Bagneesh your eeex-change student. I am here to study Eeen-glish at Eeeas-tern High School."

He had the strangest accent I'd ever heard. Sounded like the kid on the old Johnny Quest TV show.

"What part of Indiana you from, young man?"

He answered. "I am from New Delhi, the ca-peee-tal."

"New Del-hee?" Mayor Cutlip frowned. "New Delhi isn't no capital of where you're from little man. Indianapolis is the ca-peee-tal."

He had mocked his diction a bit. At that the Mayor turned to his lovely wife Mildred who was all prettied up in typical Cutlip fashion. He whispered at her: "Ain't Indianapolis the capital of Indiana?"

"Last time I checked it was," she whispered back.

Emboldened, Mayor Cutlip turned back towards Baneesh. "What you mean New Delhi is the capital?"

"I am from ca-peee-tal of Eeen-dia, New Delhi."

"India?"

He could have said Mars or Pluto. The Mayor gasped a big one and so did the whole crowd. I thought he was going to have a heart attack right on the spot but he didn't. The Mayor stepped back, held his heart like Vince Gill does when he gets his Grammy awards and said, "India? So you're from India?"

Bagneesh nodded. "Yes, sir."

Mayor Cutlip touched his cheek. "Why, the exchange service was supposed to send us someone from In..." And before he could get Indiana out he realized the exchange service had made a mistake. It was too late to correct it. Bagneesh was already there. It sure was awkward waitin' on the Mayor to figure out what to do.

Then out of nowhere, like a breath of fresh air, RoseMarie Patton, lead majorette for the Marchin' Highlanders, bought the Mayor some time by tweetin' three times on her whistle and before you knew it the band was beltin' out "Raindrops Keep Fallin' on My Head" again and everybody smiled, though awkwardly.

Mayor Cutlip thought a bit before putting his arm around Bagneesh's shoulder. He then led his guest to the speaker's platform. I felt for the Mayor.

Bagneesh walked delicate-like to the mike alongside the Mayor, who was squeezin' Bagneesh so hard I thought he was going to squoosh the juice right out of him. I asked Cliff why Bagneesh had a towel wrapped around his head and Cliff said it was because he had wet hair, but I pointed out that couldn't be the case because he'd been on the bus a full hour, if indeed he'd been on since Cincinnati, and his hair should have been dry twice over.

(Unless, of course, he'd dunked his head into the sink in the bus restroom to get it wet because of the heat.)

Bagneesh stepped to the mike. The Band stopped. The Mayor stopped squeezin'. The *News Democrat* reporter licked his pencil. Bagneesh opened his mouth, smiled nervously, and the Western band broke out in "Raindrops Keep Fallin' on My Head" all over again. We cheered, relaxed, got more goose pimples.

When he spoke we hung on his every word. "Hello, Lake Moobegon. My name is Bagneesh. I am from Eeen-dia. I like your town and I love hard candy. Thank you."

Kind of strange but we all went along with the hard candy thing. Tons of people went to the Cutlips that first week and dropped off hard candy. He liked to got tons of it: peppermint, anise, orange, peanut butter, some with squooshy insides, others dusted with sugar. All of it was good. The people in my town have always gone out of their way to make guests feel at home.

As it turned out Bagneesh couldn't stand hard candy. Later he told me he'd really said, "Hartan County" instead of "hard candy." It didn't matter because he enjoyed the attention. The Cutlips gave the hard candy out for Halloween and no one complained.

And no one cared that he was from India either. In fact I deemed it providential. Here in little ol' Lake Moobegon was a foreigner who was giving us a leg up on Martin's Sink.

Bagneesh was fun. We were the same age. The Cutlips used to drag him to high school events to make a celebrity out of him, which worked because he later became the unofficial mascot for all Eastern football and for the golf team. He helped us beat the Western Highlanders for the first time in three years. His cheers made us all laugh.

"Back 'em up, let's go Eagles, re-in-car-nate them to Beagles!"

We hadn't the slightest idea what he meant when he said it but we sure had a blast listening. By the end of football season we voted him head cheerleader over Billy Baughen and boy was he a funny sight twirlin' his baton, towel on head, black suit, beltin' out cheers. I never laughed so much in my life. Sometimes I wondered whether he even understood his own cheers.

"Knock 'em back, Highlanders sack. Beat 'em back to Bangladesh!"

My fondest memory of him was from Thanksgiving Day '73. The Cutlips had left town for two days to be in Ashtabula where they always had their holiday meal with their Grandma Cutlip. Bagneesh asked to stay behind because of a head cold. Besides, he said, he didn't eat meat.

Around two that afternoon our phone rang. Bagneesh asked if he could come over. He had been lonely sittin' in that big mansion with just Prissy, the dog. Uncle Johnny and I picked him up and before we knew it the Talbotts had their first ever foreigner over for dinner.

We spent the day huddled near Grandma Renie's coal stove while the adults watched the Lions lose to the Packers. The heat felt nice and every once in a while I would open the stove door to stoke the fire and throw in a chunk of black coal just to watch it burn.

Grandma Renie had five pumpkin pies that filled the air with a delightful smell that made my mouth water. She brought her slices piping hot with real whipped cream slidin' all over them just cryin' out to be eaten and we drank hot cocoa with tiny marshmallows on top and boy did that taste good.

I had on a wool sweater, the one Grandma Renie had made for me, which meant I was toasty warm all curled up next to the coal stove. Bagneesh rubbed his hands a bit; he wasn't used to cold air. The stove eventually warmed him up, though. It sure was funny lookin' at him wearing a Cincinnati Bengals sweatshirt, blue jeans, wool socks — all things he wouldn't have worn a few months earlier.

We talked about what we wanted out of life and he shared his dreams. It was just me and him. He talked about India, how they had a caste system, and how some people couldn't rise in society just because of the way they were born.

"America eees good," he said, "because everybody has a chance."

He told me about India's history, how the English pretty much ran things until not that far back and how Ghandi was their George Washington, except he beat the British without firin' a shot while Washington did. Strange how our two countries got independence from the same country.

We talked religion. I was more sold on mine than he on his. He said he was a Hindu but that he really hadn't swallowed it whole hog. Bein' away from his relatives had given him the opportunity to examine his beliefs in a new light. I began to tell him about Jesus Christ and to my surprise he knew a bit. He said he had learned of Jesus from a woman missionary that lived near his New Delhi home.

One thing he had a hard time understanding about Christianity was how a person could be born again and not be reincarnated. It seemed odd to him. I really didn't know how to explain it so he could understand but Grandma could. I enjoyed the time because for the first time ever I had to explain to someone all the stuff I'd learned in Sunday School.

Bagneesh wanted to go to medical school and become a doctor like his older brothers. I gathered by the way he talked that he was from a well-to-do family. He was a straight-shootin' guy though, not many airs, and a likeable sort. Could have gotten along real well in Lake Moobegon had he stayed for the duration.

After three slices of pie he loosened his belt, kicked his feet onto the coal bucket, wound his hands behind his neck and groaned. They must not eat much desert in India.

We became good friends that afternoon. After that we always waved at one another in the hallway, said Hi, and to this day trade Christmas cards. Bagneesh is a doctor. Says he can't make near the money in India that he makes here in America. Plus, he likes Vermont. He's a country doctor with a pretty wife, three teenage boys, and he spends time skiing and hiking. He's a good Joe.

TWELVE

You've probably realized by now that I haven't mentioned my parents much. That's because it's awful tough to talk about it. I wish the pain would just go away. They tell me it might someday.

Mom and Dad died the same year a couple years ago. She died first with cancer and he a month later of a heart attack. It was real sudden with them both. They were only 53. Fortunately they got to see my little Kevin before passing away. My wife's name is Sue Ann and I haven't talked much about her because she didn't come from Lake Moobegon and therefore she couldn't be in any of these stories. She's an outsider. We met in The City at a Skyline Chili restaurant near Mt. Lookout.

It was especially tough the day Mom died. She had been everything to us kids because Dad had to spend so much time at his two jobs just to keep things afloat. She spent her last days home while cancer ate her body and it made her scream. It was too much for me so I left often to go down to Ken's Barber Shoppe where the old men talked politics and the Reds. Even when the doctor gave her morphine the pain kept right up. Her only hope was in finding relief in Jesus.

When the end came we called Doc Sensabaugh and Cliff's father. Cliff Sr. felt bad when he had to put Mom in a plastic bag to take her to the funeral home. You could see Mom's death strained Dad. They'd known each other 50 years and now their marriage really was until death did them part. It was a lot harder on him than me and my brothers Billy, Steve, and Doug.

Dad died three weeks later of a broken heart and it seemed fitting. They belonged together. Folks that had come from far off to see Mom's funeral came back for Dad. Pastor Pete delivered the best sermon I'd ever heard and I wished I had it on audio tape because it sounded so good. His best lines were these: "God had a time set aside for Leroy Bennett Talbott to die, a time decided long ago. It may have been a surprise to you but nothing is a surprise to Him. Even when it seems as if He isn't in control, He is."

I've never been so thankful for Lake Moobegon, Ohio, as I was that lonely day. The town brought us covered dishes, sympathy cards, pleasant words, and they cried on our shoulders because they too all shared our pain.

Not long ago while driving from The City to visit Cliff Jr. before a football game, I decided to detour through Lake Moobegon United-In-Peace Cemetery just to sneak a peek at Mom and Dad's gravesite. The site seemed so peaceful, almost friendly, as the soft autumn wind blowed a sweet song of love into my memories of them. Even though they were gone from Earth they left me two lifetimes of love. I'm looking forward to that Great Day when I can visit up with them again.

THIRTEEN

The social hangout for most older men is Ken's Barber Shoppe. I learned all about life there. Some men sit there all day. Ken is closed on Sundays and after three on Wednesday so he can take his mother to the Riplet quilter's group. The men at Ken's discuss important world issues and how to solve them.

(There was once talk of Ken joinin' forces with Madge from Monica's Hair Loft in order to cut down on rent, but Ken's men would have nothin' to do with him if he had. They told him they would start goin' to the Martin's Sink barber if they had to because they said they got enough jabberin' from their wives at home, let alone havin' to suffer through it all over again at the Hair Loft. I guess it's one thing to live with your wife, it's another to get your hair cut with her.)

Politicians could learn more about the real world if they had to visit Ken's every week. It would put life in perspective for them. Conversations there seem scripted at times. The men usually start with the weather, then go on to the Reds. Sometimes they talk about their house. Eventually the conversation swings to politics in Columbus and Washington.

"Do any of you know what the weather's s'posed to be like this week?" asked Ben Rupp, brushin' a clump of cut hair off his pants leg.

"Don't quite know if I ought to plant, yet."

Ken snipped stray hair sproutin' from Ben's nose. "The weatherman on Channel 12 says it's supposed to be sunny. Of course, he said it was goin' to be sunny last week but look what happened. Rained like Noah's ark."

Ben's voice began droning a bit, matching Ken's electric shaver. "Radio says there's a chance of showers on Wednesday."

"The Farmer's Almanac says it's okay to plant," stated Sam Cartwright in the "next" chair. He was chewin' a killer wad of Red Man, in line for the next cut.

Ben Rupp brushed away a hair tickling his cheek. "Farmer's Almanac said that?"

"Yep."

Ken clipped twice. A long moment later, he veered the topic off into another direction. "Anyone hear how the Reds did?"

"Lost," came Sam. "Three-two. Harnisch gave up three solo shots. They need more pitchin'. Better relievers if you ask me. And a closer."

Ken began trimmin' Ben's neck with an electric trimmer. "I think they need a power hitter," he said as his hands and voice vibrated in tandem. "Signin' those high-priced free agents don't cut it. Nobody's worth the kind of money those players get. Some of them make more in one month than I'll make in a lifetime. And they don't know how to fix a tractor, either."

"I say they're worth it if people pay it. It's supply and demand."

"I suppose."

On cue Fred Wardlaw squeaked open the door and headed for a padded seat next to the kerosene heater. Ruff, Ken's basset hound, waggin' his tail like no tomorrow, lay sprawled out by the stove near the hair clippings. Fred had to move to The City a while back to work at Cincinnati Milacron. He still drives 40 miles once every two weeks to get his hair cut. His wife goes to Monica because it's tough to break an old habit.

"Fred, how you been doin'," waved Ben as he looked at Fred in the mirror on the back wall. "Last time I seen you was a year ago. What you been up to?"

"How do, Ben, Ken, Sam. Me and Kate done moved to a house down near The City. It's beautiful, hardwood floors and all."

"Where you moved to?"

"Down near Beechmont way."

"Is that so?"

Fred blinks. "Yep. Those hardwood floors are real nice."

Ken said, "I knowed a man down New Hope way who'll put them floors in for you. How'd you get yours done?"

"We hired this outfit down at Beechmont that specializes in that sort of thing. They actually come in and lay the whole floor in one day."

Ken nodded his approval. "Is that so? I heard about a special process like that on Paul Harvey?"

"That's the one," said Fred.

"Then it must be good."

"They do it for a mite reasonable price now, too."

"Do they polyurethane?"

Fred narrowed his eyes. "That polyurethane is a whole different story. You see, polyurethane has to go on in coats and it takes more than a day to do it. So if you want that done you got to pay extra. Shoot, I did it myself. Saved a bundle."

Well, that's what I'd do," said Sam as he reached down to scratch Ruff's ear. "No use payin' someone when you can do it just as good yourself."

Fred glanced around the room to make eye contact with someone, anyone, and ended up catching Ben. "Now that would be nice if they included polyurethane in the price," he said.

"Boy, that would be a good."

Ben began counting his fingers. "Well, you got to figure labor for two, cost of brushes, polyurethane. That doesn't come cheap. Not to mention tyin' up the house until it dries."

A half hour later after all that "floor" talk there was a silence and not long after that Ken shouted "Next!" Folks here talk about important things like hardwood floors, sewer pipes, kitchen cabinets or whether the state will close the Lake Moobegon exit on the Appalachian Highway.

Ken drew his lips inward, shook his head. "Kind of think that would be the death of this town. No exit, no business."

Fred sighed and jammed a clean plug of Red Man into his waiting mouth. "I don't understand with the economy the way it is why they don't keep that exit open," he mumbled, a bulge forming.

"Well, now they claim makin' it limited access will bring more trucks through the area and that'll be good for business," said Ben. "Of course, I don't really know what to believe."

Sam offered his two cents. "Well it'll be great for Pickle's Cove because their exit's goin' to stay open. Don't think those boys in Columbus really know what's up."

"Betcha they're making it limited access so some friend of the Governor can get part of the action. I wonder if the Governor done got himself some interest in Pickle's Cove?"

With his belly scrapin' the floor, Ruff the Dog waddled over towards Fred who scratched him behind the ear again. Fred dribbled over the dog and into a spittoon. "That's what's wrong with government," he said, "they just don't know what's right for us little people. If they'd only get off their duffs and get down here they'd know what we really needed."

"Ben piped in. "That's as likely to happen as Marge Schott sellin' the Reds."

"It's those politicians in Washington who are messin' us to pieces," Ken said. "Why, they all ought to be tossed out. The whole lot of 'em. Can't trust any of 'em. Why, if it was up to me..."

At this point Fred turned and spat another slobber of tobacco juice into Ken's brass spittoon, *ker-plunk*. Most men in Lake Moobegon prefer Red Man over Mail Pouch. They say it's moister, though some have been known to go out of their way to buy Mail Pouch. I tried it once but swallowed the plug and turned green so I have a good reason to abstain.

Chewin' tobacky is the townspeople's only real vice. I've wondered if the men do it because they truly enjoy it or because they feel like they should support tobacco. If it weren't for tobacco many Lake Moobegoners would have to work in The City. Of course, not many of them would like to work in a factory or else they'd done it years ago.

"Did you say it was supposed to rain tomorrow?"

"Like cats and dogs."

"Great. Means I can come back for a trim. Plantin' can wait."

FOURTEEN

Lake Moobegon has quite a few folks with special talents. Folks from Martin's Sink call these people circus freaks but I think they're just jealous. Two folks in particular are Billy Fender and his amazing leg, and the famous singin' team of Elmer and Ireta Wardlaw. I'm sure you've heard of the Wardlaws.

My first knowledge of Billy Fender's leg goes way back to when I was in Seventh Grade. At the time my Billy was in Tenth Grade and was a close friend of my brother Doug.

One Saturday Billy and Doug went huntin' in Balle County and took along our twin beagles, Scout and Arrow, to track rabbits. After a couple hours of catchin' nothin', they got bogged down in a marsh. It got dark and before you knew it they were lost. (I've known my brother my whole life and have never known him to get lost. He has always been good with directions after passing Map Orientation as a Second Class Boy Scout. I guess just about anyone can get lost in life when they're not payin' attention.)

Billy and Doug knew from where they were that they had to go north to get to where they wanted to be because they'd headed south from Billy's car to start things off. Only problem was it was so cloudy they couldn't follow the North Star and they'd forgotten to bring a compass along and they didn't have a map either. Lost in Balle County with Billy Fender and two stubborn beagles, Scout and Arrow, and no food except a crumbled Planters Peanut Bar that Doug had trouble digging out of his pocket and once he did the lint mixed in with the peanuts, which made it inedible, of course.

Then Billy Fender began to reveal his incredible gift. He said: "Doug, lay your jacket on the ground."

Doug narrowed his gaze. "What you say?"

"I said lay your jacket on the ground."

"Why? You goin' to take a nap."

"No stupid. I'm goin' to get us out of here."

"Can you make that jacket fly?"

Billy looked Doug straight in the eyes. "No, Doug, I'm going to steer us home."

At that Billy made Doug swear he'd never tell anyone. (Later I found a book with Doug's handwriting and read the story about Billy's leg before I realized it was his diary. Then I put it away. Therefore, technically, he never broke his promise.)

According to the diary Billy broke his leg playin' tackle football for the Eastern JV football team. It was such a bad break they had to put a steel rod in it to give the bone more strength. Billy's mom and dad, owners of Fender's IGA, had made the mistake of sending Billy to Hartan County General which left Billy's future up to the brain trust there. True to form, a doctor there outfitted Billy with an experimental magnetic rod instead of the standard steel one.

Billy didn't realize he had a magnetic leg until it started doin' crazy things. Coins were stickin' to it and he was draggin' metal cans off grocery shelves as he walked by. That last one was tough for Billy because he often worked as a stocker at his father's grocery. The doctors told him he had to wear the rod for four years; it couldn't come out until he was 20.

"What do you mean you can steer us home?"

"You remember back about a year ago, when my leg broke?"

"Uh-huh."

"Well, the clods at Hartan County General did it to me. They put a magnetic rod in my leg to strengthen it."

"Weren't they supposed to put a rod in?"

"No, stupid. They weren't suppose to put a magnetic one in. My leg has strange powers."

"Powers?" (At this juncture I can imagine Doug opening his eyes wide in wonder, as if he were eyeing a UFO or Marge Schott for the first time.)

"Yes, powers. I can do things normal folks can't. Remember when I joined the radio class at school? They had to kick me out because everytime my leg got near an audiotape it'd erase the whole blasted thing. They called me Mr. Degausser. My leg's a magnet!"

"No!" breathed in Doug.

"Yessirree, Bob! And when I walk past a canned corn display at the grocery the whole thing comes tumblin' down. My leg pulls 'em."

"Are you pullin' my leg?"

"Nope," he said. "Watch this."

And that was when Billy laid himself down on Doug's jacket and waited and waited and waited and finally his leg moved like a Ouija board thing. After fifteen minutes, Billy looked right satisfied and stood up. Doug couldn't believe what he had seen.

"There you go! That's north!"

"What do you mean, that's north?"

"That's north. Now let's go!"

Sure enough, ol' Billy Fender's leg was a magnet and before long they found U.S. 62 and from there they hiked back to Billy's father's pick-up and drove home as if nothing had happened. Miracle from God if you ask me.

A year or two later Billy began showing off his leg and before you knew it he was doin' magic tricks for kids at Hartan County General and makin' them laugh so hard milk would come out their nose. Classic example of takin' a handicap and makin' it a blessin' to others.

He has this one trick where he mysteriously makes a spoon move across a table without strings and it has all the kids oooin' and aawin'. Of course, I knowed how he done it because I'd read the diary.

Elmer Wardlaw and sister Ireta are different. They were born with their talent. In my opinion they are the best singers that have ever graced the halls of Eastern High School.

Lake Moobegon was too small for Elmer. His talents propelled him to the very pinnacle of his profession as a music teacher at Walnut Hills High School in The City. Occasionally he comes back to Lake Moobegon Church of Christ and does concerts with sister Ireta, the last concert a benefit for new hand fans. When they sing they pack them in like sardines. Ireta is the music teacher at Pickle's Cove but we love her anyway.

Elmer has the best soprano voice in the world. Freak of nature if you ask me but he sounds so pretty warblin' away folks don't mind a bit. Yes, he could feel sorry for himself for bein' a male soprano but that has never been Elmer's way.

Folks here have decided he's a cross between Bing Crosby and Olivia Newton John. The girls don't mind. In fact for a while before he got married, Elmer was one of the most eligible bachelors Lake Moobegon ever had.

Ireta, on the other hand, sings alto. When you put the two of them together you can almost hear the gates of heaven open. Saint Peter, here I come! When the Wardlaws sing it's an event. I liken it to the L.M.U.M.C.A.A.I.C.F. and July Fourth all rolled up into one. A whole gaggle of married women show, a fact that has made more than one husband jealous. It's not Elmer's fault he sings so pretty. He doesn't ask for the women, they just flock to him the way ants smell picnic. Elmer isn't that good-lookin' but one women I talked with says it's his voice that makes her and so many others go crazy. In other words he's really more an Elvis Presley or Billy Ray Cyrus.

Elmer's voice is so high he even broke glass one night during the Baptismal Pond Concert at Lake Moobegon Church of Christ. Right at the end of He Lives! where you have to hit that high G, Elmer actually went an octave higher than he was supposed to and cracked the church's stained glass window below the picture of baby Jesus in the manger where "In memory of Juliet Holstein 1899-1934" is.

We were just sittin' there feelin' the tension as the high note hit and then *pop*! *pow*! Ireta screamed bloody murder. Pastor Pete jumped like a bunny rabbit. I jumped. No one knew what had happened. Then Shorty McGuire, who was next to baby Jesus, shouted "Elmer done broke the glass!" and then there was an uncomfortable silence.

Elmer felt bad and we all felt bad because he felt bad then he felt bad because we felt bad because he felt bad. It wasn't his fault that God gave him such a powerful voice.

A month later he and Ireta came back, this time for a benefit to replace the cracked stained glass. I thought he'd gone loco when near the end of the benefit he went off on his own, without Ireta, a cappella, to sing "I serve a risen Saviour, He's in the world today" which is the opening line from He Lives!

You could see Pastor Pete squirmin' once he realized it. Even though Elmer was singin' like only Elmer can, nobody was paying much attention to him and his high voice. This time we were all lookin' at the stained glass and baby Jesus, wonderin' if the glass would snap to pieces like a dry Saltine. My palms were gettin' sweaty.

Finally Elmer crooned: "You ask me how I know he lives" — it was the next to last line, and the air was thick with tension. Then he sang, "He lives (high note!) within my heart!"

It turned out he didn't sing the really high note but the regular high G instead. Pastor Pete breathed a heavy sigh and everyone applauded and went nuts and it was the greatest musical finale that could have been heard this side of heaven. The tension had been nigh incredible. I tell you, Elmer sure can spellbound an audience. He is the greatest example I know of someone who has taken a freak thing and turned it around for everyone's benefit.

FIFTEEN

LeRoy The Music Salesman traveled all over rural southern Ohio, delivering musical instruments and accesories to the high schools there. He visited Eastern High School at least once a month and I got my first flutophone off him. Nobody knew his last name — he was just LeRoy The Music Salesman. We all liked him and he provided a valuable service. Hartan County was so tiny it couldn't support a music store and so LeRoy The Music Salesman was its music store.

The Big Dream of Eastern's music teacher, Mr. Ray Mignerey, was to have a real marching band called The Eastern High Flyin' Eagle Marching Band and Drill Team. He wanted to march every Fourth of July down Old Cincinnati Road instead of having to watch those Western Highlanders do it. Ray wanted a band real bad but didn't know how to raise money; band uniforms and instruments cost lots. Enter LeRoy.

"Mr. Mignerey, do I have a fund raiser for you?" gushed Leroy, his black hair slicker than a lamb at birth.

Ray paused. "Whatcha got LeRoy?"

"You ever tried sellin' postcards?"

"Postcards?"

"Yeah, you know, the things you buy when you're on a vacation so folks'll know where you have been?"

"Why do we need postcards?"

"You can sell 'em to raise money for band uniforms. What if I told you that for every postcard you sell you get fifty cents."

"Fifty cents?"

"And that can all be yours. Here's how it works...."

LeRoy proceeded to enlighten Mr. Mignerey about all the wonderful benefits of sellin' scenic Hartan County postcards and how people would be knockin' down doors to buy them and how with all the passerbys at the Gas & Go in Lake Moobegon they could sell hundreds, maybe even thousands.

"Just stack 'em high and watch 'em fly," he said. LeRoy related how a band in West Virginia bought postcards and raised five thousand dollars and how they all ended up with felt hats and white spats.

It got Mr. Mignerey's brain whirrin' like a cuckoo clock.

Next visit, as a personal favor, LeRoy said he'd give five cents of his own commission away for every postcard sold just to see the sale made. When Mr. Mignerey wavered at that, oh my, LeRoy opened up his own personal checkbook and wrote a check out to The Eastern Band Fund for $50. Right there on the spot. Enough said. Sold. LeRoy The Music Salesman wasn't dumb because he knew if Eastern raised money for a band they'd end up buyin' their musical instruments off him and he'd end up with a windfall.

Mr. Mignerey broke the news at the next PTA meeting and excitement from his announcement caused a stampede of ideas. Everybody liked it. Even Billy Fender's mother said, "About time we got a band." Mr Mignerey went on to explain how Hartan County postcards would be the rage and sold at stores and door-to-door by students and sold at each exit of the James A. Rhodes Appalachian Highway and on a rack at the Gas & Go.

Then Mr. Mignerey explained how only one glossy picture could be chosen for the postcard. Leroy The Music Salesman had made it quite clear to him that there could be only one postcard.

One group of parents headed by Cliff's cousin, Bobby Joe, felt a glossy of the Riplet Tobacco Warehouse was most appropriate. This group was made up of tobacco farmin' parents who wanted postcards to promote their livelihood. They felt tobacco was bein' put down too much and needed good press. They even suggested havin' a picture of a little green tobacco worm named "Orville" tucked into the corner of the postcard sayin' "Greetings from Tobacco Land!" This group also had the backing of the business community, which included Brian the Head Teller and Alverna.

Another group desired a picture of Andy Holbrook's birthplace along with his minor league averages and height/weight/bats/throws on back. Andy was a legend they said, the first inductee into the Hartan County Hall of Fame and to many Babe Ruth reincarnate. This faction was led by Andy's teammates at Lake Moobegon Church of Christ. They believed that with the popularity of baseball cards that an Andy Holbrook postcard might become a true collector's item.

Both sides had good points.

It turned ugly. At one point both sides started shoutin' at one another, bein' un-Lake Moobegon-like. Eventually Mr. Dunn, Old Ben's son and PTA president, had to step in and ask for a vote, but since most parents were gone by then because the meeting had drifted past midnight both sides soon agreed to postpone any vote until the next meeting.

But then Mr. Dunn had another idea. Perhaps, he suggested, the vote should be placed on the November ballot along with the vote for U.S. President. It seemed to make sense — let the ballot box decide. That motion was seconded, quorum was met, barely, and it passed. Before you knew it we had Proposition 4B and the ugliest political campaign ever held in Hartan County. And all over a stupid postcard.

You'd never thought it possible for there to be so much animosity in a school district but in Fall 1977 animosity was it. Both sides organized committees, printed posters, folks went door-to-door, rallies were held. One bake sale featured "Orville-the-Tobacco-Worm" tobacco-flavored cookies that were two steps below disgusting.

On October 30 an Andy Holbrook Rally was held on the steps of Lake Moobegon Church of Christ where Pastor Pete came this close to likening a vote for Andy as a vote for God. Andy didn't show for his own rally. Some said he didn't like the attention.

Andy deserved bein' on that postcard. Pastor Pete said these memorable words at the rally: "While a senior at Eastern High School our favorite son, Andy Holbrook, broke all records and led the Hartan County High School Baseball League, HCHSBL, with seventeen out-of-park home runs. He later went on to bigger things as a professional baseball player, playing for Cedar Rapids, Butte, Jefferson City, Kenosha, Tri-Cities, Bluefield, Oklahoma City, and the Spokane Spokes. He was only a few days away from bein' called up to the Majors when he was hit on the left eye by a fastball thrown by Curt Vegas of the Fresno Forty-Niners. His career ended that day, July seventeenth, nineteen hundred and sixty-three. Even though it's been a while Andy's memory lives on in the hearts and minds of his friends and acquaintances."

A few younger women bawled. I fought tears. Big Andy had been a great one, our claim to fame, and I was going to do all I could to get his picture on the front of that postcard in order to defeat tobacco and its evil juice that was staining my beloved hero's memory.

It almost seemed like God was on our side. If you added up that Andy was a believer in Jesus, plus the fact tobacco, as a weed, had done so much damage to so many people, certainly even God would have to come to the conclusion that a vote for Andy was a vote for Him.

I loved Big Andy.

Pastor Pete blinked at a tear, his voice choked with emotion: "Andy was Lake Moobegon's ambassador to the world. He worked hard. He always gave one hundred percent and never asked for anything in return. Just like Pete Rose. Big Andy was an example to youth. He is a member of our church. We should do everything within our power to make sure he wins one last game, the game of being on that postcard to raise money for the band."

"Preach it, brother."

"And furthermore, I hope every one of you shows support for your brother in Christ by voting for him this fall."

I had goose pimples. It was the greatest speech I'd ever heard. Felt like I'd died and gone to be with the Lord. So now all I had to do was persuade all my friends to vote for Andy. Jesus' disciples started with Jerusalem, so I would start with Cliff.

"What you mean you're not votin' for Andy? He's practically near a saint as you can get. He's the greatest sports legend Lake Moobegon has ever produced. You can't *can't* vote for him."

"Bobby Joe is my cousin and blood is thicker than water. I've already given my pledge to him that I'll support Tobacco and that's final."

"You mean you want a little green tobacco juice suckin' worm named Orville tellin' folks they're welcome to TobaccoLand? Are you nuts?"

"I don't like that little green worm any better than you like it. But tobacco is important to Lake Moobegon and besides I just don't think it's right to dote over a man the way you're dotin' over Andy. He's just flesh and bone. You're treatin' him like he's Saint Andrew or somethin'."

"You know I'm not doin' that."

"Are too."

"Are not."

"Are."

"Not."

"Andy Holbrook put Lake Moobegon on the map. Nobody knows we even grow tobacco here and nobody cares. Tobacco is bad for you anyway."

"Nobody knows about our tobacco because we haven't advertised it," he said. "Put that little green worm on a postcard with a bale of burley and I bet you City tourists will be flockin' to Riplet like Arabs to Mecca and before you know it we'll have a major tourist attraction with people comin' in from all over the world. We'll have to build an airport by golly. Just you wait and see."

I flicked a finger at Cliff's face. "If we put Andy on the postcard folks'll be flockin' to Riplet anyway to see his plaque next to the AT&T pay phone at the Hartan County Hall of Fame. So what's the difference?"

"The difference is blood is thicker than water."

Cliff was so close I could smell his breath. He'd had onions for dinner. I said, "I know who my friends are."

"And I know who my friends are."

Cliff was bein' a hardhead again and there was nothin' I could do to stop him since he'd made up his mind and once Cliff makes up his mind to be a hardhead he won't change.

Had a real fallin' out over the postcard. Things never really got right until about four months after the election. Our relationship suffered more over that stupid green worm than with what had happened with the feed mill fight. The tobacco people won 2246 to 2026, but as it turned out the vote didn't matter. Three weeks after the election LeRoy The Music Salesman got promoted and forgot to leave a forwarding address. His mail came back Return To Sender. Nobody knew how to get in touch with the postcard people. Mr. Mignerey was a mite upset the way things went, not just because he didn't get the band outfitted but because he was an Andy booster. The vote soured him on the idea of a band. He told Brian the Head Teller that Eastern didn't deserve one.

A year later Mr. Mignerey transferred to Western and now he leads their marching band on July Fourth. I wonder if he's really at peace with himself.

SIXTEEN

I learned about East Coast culture the week my family went on summer vacation in '75 to Washington, D.C.. Most folks in Lake Moobegon don't give a hoot about vacations because they don't see any need for them. People usually go on vacations to get away from it all. Here in Hartan County folks are already away from it all. So why go.

It's hard to explain the looks I got when I told Cliff we were going. Billy Fender called me stupid and said the fishin' was better right here. I told him to go break a leg.

I think East Coast folks are just plain rude. They don't say, "How do?" when they meet you on the sidewalk and they don't smile. They're always rushin' around like snakes with their heads cut off, writhin' from one lane on the superhighway to the next in their fancy red foreign cars. Why don't they just drive in one lane and stay put? They don't wave when they meet you on a two-lane and the worst thing is their lack of common sense. Let me give you an example.

Around Cincinnati we have this habit of sayin' "please?" when we can't hear what you have said. It comes from the German word "bitte." Please is the polite way to say "I can't hear you."

In Washington, D.C. they say, "Huh?" or "Whadya say?" It's impolite but that's Easterners for you.

While takin' that vacation in '75 Dad got intrigued by a McDonald's restaurant we passed near Washington, D.C., so he slammed on his brakes, pulled over and made a U-turn to get back to it. Dad had always wanted to go through a drive-thru restaurant because he'd never been through one. The mere thought of it had been nigh an obsession. So he turned into the parkin' lot and got in the drive-thru line. None of us knew what to expect. I was tense.

I asked Dad, "How do they do it?"

"Yeah, how do they do it?" Mom chimed in. "Do they have someone come out to your car or do they take the order when you get up to the window?"

Dad scratched his head. "Beats me. I'm just goin' to follow the car ahead and see what he does. I expect they done did it before."

Little Billy had to put in his two cents worth. "How do we know what to order? We never been here. Do they have vanilla cones with jimmies?"

"I don't rightly expect so but they may."

Thirty seconds later we were in the same spot. Mom said to Dad, "I don't see anyone comin' out. Do you think we should get out to see what's goin' on?"

"I do believe that's a right nice idea. Come on everybody. We need to stretch our legs anyway. Let's see what's happenin'."

So we all got out and just as we did the car in front inched forward. Kind of startled us. So we all got back in and Dad moved forward, too. When the car in front stopped again we noticed a sign with the entire McDonald's menu on it to our left, including how much everything was. They had Big Macs, fries, quarter pounders, all the stuff we'd heard about but had never had the chance to eat. After a minute of gawkin' at the menu the strangest thing happened. It was a voice from the netherworld.

"Cccch...Welcome to McDonald's. May I take your order please?"

Dad spun around at me. "What did you say? Your voice sounds a mite scratchy, Danny."

"I didn't say nothin'."

"Ccccch...Welcome to McDonalds, may I ccccch...take your order please?"

"There it goes again," Dad exclaimed, now pointin' out his window at the menu board where he thought the noise was coming from. He was about to have a kniption fit. "Why that noise is comin' from the menu board!"

"Ccccch...Welcome to McDonald's, may I ccccch....take your order, please?"

"Hello? Someone there? Where are you? We can't see you."

"Ccccch... Sir, I'm talking to you through the speaker. Do you see that box with the wire screen across it....Ccccch....right next to your window?"

The stupid box was right in front of Dad's face. "Yes, I see it," he said.

"That's the speaker. If you'll t——- me what you w——t, Ccccch... I'll g——ly order it for you."

The man in the box didn't sound none too good. Mom said, "I can barely understand him. Could you tell him to repeat what he just said?"

Dad gave his best effort. "Sir, could you repeat what you just said?"

"CCCCCH...I SAID IF YOU JUST TELL ME WHAT YOU WANT, CCCCCH...I'LL GLADLY ORDER IT FOR YOU. THERE... CCCCCH... CAN YOU HEAR ME, NOW?"

We had to scrape Mom off the ceiling. Dad knocked his head against the ceilin', his knee hit the horn. *Beep*. We all laughed real hard. McDonald's sure was fun.

Dad collected himself enough to answer. "Hello? Yes, we hear you. Could you turn that there speaker down a hair? You nearly blowed our socks off!"

At this point I was gigglin' so hard I couldn't stop.

"Sorry, sir."

Dad asked, "What's the house specialty? Whatever it is, I want six of 'em and we also want six Pepsis."

"Sir, we sell Coke. Ccccccch...will that be okay? And our specialty is the Big Mac."

"Coke's no problem. We'll have six Big Macs then."

"And cccch....do you cccch... .want any... .ccccccch.....with that sir."

"Please?" asked Dad, wanting his to repeat would he'd said. The speakerman could have asked if we wanted eighteen thousand gray elephants and a rhino for desert for all we knew.

"That'll be ten dollars and fifty-three cents. Pull up to the first window."

Now we figured $10.95 was a lot to pay for six Big Macs and Pepsis, yet we didn't want to be impolite, especially since this was our first visit to Mr. McDonald's restaurant. So we swallowed our pride, paid, started up the road. But we noticed something strange. We had more food than we'd ordered. Four bags was way too much.

"Look at this, they gave us six cherry pies," said Mom.

"Six cherry pies?"

"We paid for 'em too. They're on the receipt."

Dad eyed the receipt and got so angry you could almost hear his blood boiling. Flames were poppin' out his ears. "So they think they can take advantage of us hicks, now do they?" (This was almost the angriest I'd ever seen him. Once when Brooks Robinson robbed Johnny Bench in the '70 World Series by catchin' a ball backhanded and throwin' him out by a half step, Dad threw a paperweight and broke a lava lamp.)

Dad U-turned, floored the car all the way to the restaurant, marched inside. He wasn't about to be stuck payin' for six cherry pies he didn't order.

"Sir, our order takin' clerk swears he heard you say 'please' after he asked you whether you wanted extra cherry pies. If you don't want them you shouldn't have ordered them."

"But I said 'please.'"

"So you wanted them!"

"No I didn't!"

"Just take this and go."

He handed Dad three bucks. "Just go!"

Dad didn't want the free pies but the manager insisted that he take them. So we ate the stupid pies. I got cherry stains on my teeth and the sugary crust flaked all over my jeans. I learned from the experience that people in Washington, D.C., speak a different language.

SEVENTEEN

I made a vow in '71 to my oldest brother that if I ever wrote a book he wouldn't be in it. I am honoring that vow. What he did irked me. One wintry afternoon he poured sorghum molasses all over me and wrapped me in White Cloud toilet tissue and tied me naked to the seat of Fred Wardlaw's outhouse during a snowstorm and I had Asiatic flu and missed three days of school. I told him then and there that I was going to leave him out of my first book. This is my first book. I might write about him in the next book. My other brothers are Billy and Doug. They never did anything to me but since they are the brothers of my older brother and therefore guilty by association I'm savin' my experiences with them for the next book, too.

EIGHTEEN

During the Civil War a legend developed in Lake Moobegon. In fact, when marketing gurus Merle and Ethel Evans opened their pizza joint on South Main Street in '82 they decided to name their business after that legend. And his name? Possum Pete.

Back in the spring of 1862 bands of mounted Confederates led by a Colonel Morgan ravaged the hills of southern Ohio, destroyin' bridges and the like, preparin' the way, they thought, for an invasion of southern Ohio. (At least that's what Grandma Renie told us.) That invasion never occurred. The Rebel advance stopped short of Cincinnati and we were forever spared of havin' a southern accent and eatin' grits and watchin' stock car racin' on T-V.

March 4, 1862: After Colonel Morgan forded the Ohio River at Maysville, Kentucky, he entered Lake Moobegon on a foggy pre-dawn mornin' from up the Old Cincinnati Road. When he got to where the four-way stop now is, his eyes looked northward and he spied the covered bridge that spanned White Oak Creek on North Main Street — at least, that's what Ben Dunn's grandfather once told Old Ben over a game of checkers at an I.O.O.F. lodge meeting in 1948.

Morgan's eyes lit up at the sight of an unburnt covered bridge and he rode like the wind and once he got there guess who was waitin' for him? Why, none other than Possum Pete. Of course back then he wasn't Possum Pete, just an old

119

possum stalling southern progress. The way the legend goes, Morgan growled at the furry creature, pulled out his pistol, and took aim. *Blam*! The bullet's force blew the varmint down. Ben Dunn's grandfather gasped at the sight from behind an oak tree. Then the Rebs lit these torches and walked under the bridge canopy as if to burn the bridge.

As if from the grave, Possum Pete suddenly arose from the dead, hissed, and forced the Rebs with the fiery torches back. Scared them and Ben Dunn's grandfather half-to-death. Even with a bullet hole in him Pete was holding off a company of Reb cavalry.

Morgan got angry with his men. He pulled his sword from its scabbard and began galloping right up to Pete. "Be gone, ye northern varmint!" Instantly he sliced him in half and kicked his dead body into White Oak Creek. Poor Pete. A Union martyr.

The story doesn't end there. Ever since then folks have sworn they have seen an old possum with a scar on its neck scamperin' across that bridge, always on a spring morning when the fog's super-thick. Kind of the way it was when Morgan killed him. They say Pete hangs out where the old covered bridge was — it's a concrete bridge now — as if he's still fightin' the Rebs.

This makes for a good campfire story.

Cliff and I got the bright idea when we're both 10 to sneak out one early March morning to see if we could catch Pete and then we'd be famous. It would have been like catchin' Big Foot or Loch Ness Monster. We figured we could catch him and open up a "Possum Pete World Museum" and sell tickets for three dollars and that way we'd be rich as well as famous. Might even attract folks from as far away as Maysville, Kentucky, or Huntington, West Virginia. If Pete obliged we could also open a petting zoo, charge 50 cents and make even more money by sellin' Grandma Renie's strawberries.

I don't know what we figured on doin' with all that money.

I remember that night as if it was yesterday: March 11, 1968. I snuck down our back steps and out the kitchen door. Outside, the fog was thicker than sorghum boiled three times. After stumblin' down our lane I walked through our corn field and rambled up Bean Road. I was supposed to meet Cliff at 3:18 a.m. behind the Bachmann's tobacco barn just north of White Oak Bridge.

And Cliff was there, waiting. He was wearing his Tony the Tiger decoder ring and holding his Uncle Jim's snake net, which was like a butterfly net except it was made of green canvas. I was wearin' my Tony the Tiger watch and 3-D glasses I got from Lucky Charms for three boxtops.

From Bachmann's barn we dashed tree to tree, duckin' behind forsythia bushes, crawlin' over and around huge boulders. I tripped on a tree root, ouch, hurt my toe and scraped my elbow. Cliff looked funny draggin' that net around but we both knew the net was an absolute necessity if we had any shot at all of capturing ol' Pete and being world famous.

We ran to the big ash tree that rests on the edge of Bachmann's farm. I licked my finger and held it out to gauge the wind direction, which was crucial. It was blowin' from the southeast. *Hmm*. Therefore we began sneaking up to the bridge from the northwest. That way old Pete couldn't smell us.

About this time I really had to go to the bathroom.

From there we crawled on hands and knees to the roots of a sycamore tree that had a wrinkled trunk soakin' water by the creek. This was where we waited: 30 feet from the bridge, upstream, on the right bank.

Time dragged on. We waited in silence. We used hand motions to communicate. About 4:00 a.m. a car scooted by, headlights gleamin'. An owl hooted. Fog thicker than thrice-boiled sorghum. We couldn't see the other creek bank. That's when we looked at each other with eyes wide as saucers. We both knew instinctively that this was The Night. I had goose pimples.

About 5:00 a.m. I noticed movement. Slow at first. Dark furry animal on the bridge. I nudged Cliff and he nudged back. (I REALLY had to go to the bathroom.) Cliff motioned for me to step towards the bridge and we walked forward. He lifted the net over his head. I held my breath. We walked tip-toes. Neither of us made a sound. Tension was incredible.

Pete was on our side of the bridge, next to the guard rail. Only 10 feet away. Pete turned, saw us. Big red eyes. Stared right through my soul. History in the makin'. It was all in slo-motion. Cliff made his move. He slammed the net down hard to nail Pete. I got out of control with excitement while Cliff held the net down.

"Ya-hoo!" I screamed. "We got the dumb thing! Ya-hoo, we're rich! Cliff, we got old Pete!" I began jumpin' up and down, yellin', then I got up on the guard rail, started to walk across it, fell off, tore up my knee but I didn't care.

Cliff got angry. "Shut up! You're goin' to wake the whole town!"

"But Cliff. We got Pete. Don't you understand?"

I was holdin' the sides of my head just takin' in the moment like I couldn't believe what had just happened. This was truly WORLD HISTORY, the greatest moment in Lake Moobegon history ever, and I was part of it. I was going to be rich and famous at the same time.

Cliff wasn't sold. "We still got to get him to my house where I can put him in the dog cage. Otherwise, we got nothin'."

Right when Cliff finished his sentence we heard a *whirr-whirr-whirr*, saw bright headlights and before you knew it an Ohio State Trooper was lookin' at us through his windshield all hairy eyeball-like while he was talking on his CB radio. Scared me half-to-death. I shook like a leaf. Even though I knowed we hadn't done nothing wrong, seein' an Ohio State Trooper at 5:00 a.m. caused me to get real afraid because it must have looked like we were doing something wrong.

The Ohio State Trooper uncurled himself from his patrol car and as he marched towards us his big black boots made a *clip-clop*, *clip-clop* with each step. Cliff later told me he thought the Trooper would have shot us if we had ran.

The Ohio State Trooper stood eight foot tall, like Goliath. "Can I help you, gentlemen?" he bellowed.

"We're fine, sir," said Cliff with more than a hint of nervousness.

The State Trooper stood over Cliff. He said, "Whatcha got in that there bag?"

"I said, "We got Possum Pete, sir." Now I *REALLY REALLY* had to go to the bathroom.

"Possum Pete?"

"Possum Pete, sir," we said together, nodding our heads in tandem like one of those plastic beagles that sit on car dashboards.

After adjusting his hat brim, the State Trooper asked, "What you boys doin' out so late? Do your parents know where you are?"

We were both too afraid to answer. So we didn't.

The Ohio State Trooper looked right through me, and snorted like a bull. "Delinquents," he spat. Glaring over at Cliff's net, he added, "Now let me see what you got in there."

Cliff scuffed the ground with his shoe. "Sir, if you look he might get away." He then got all teary-eyed and started blabbering. "Please, please, don't look," he cried. "This here is Possum Pete and he's our ticket to fame and fortune. We're goin' to be famous but not if you let him get away."

"Is that so?"

Before Cliff realized what was happening, the Ohio State Trooper grabbed the handle to Cliff's net and lifted it so quick I liked to died. Underneath was the Bachmann's barn cat: Tootsie.

"Ha-ha-ha!" chuckled the Ohio State Trooper. "So this is the possum that will make you famous." He rocked back on his feet and let out a roar from deep within his gut and the entire White Oak Valley shook. Tootsie just meowed and curled around Cliff's leg.

The Ohio State Trooper drove Cliff home first and Cliff Sr. grounded Cliff Jr. for two months. The Ohio State Trooper took me home and Dad grounded me for three months and six months of Saturdays. The worst part of it came later when in the *News Democrat* that Thursday listed under "Police Beat" was this: "Two juveniles from Lake Moobegon apprehended on White Oak Bridge, May 11, 5:00 a.m., while tryin' to catch Possum Pete. Caught Bachmann's cat by mistake."

From that moment on we vowed never to utter a word about it to another livin' bein' until we turned 18. We also vowed never to dig for gold, seek out UFOs, search for hidden treasure or look for Possum Pete again. It's risky business believin' in old wives' tales.

NINETEEN

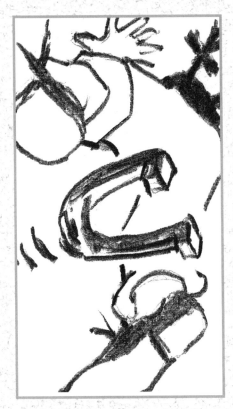

If you listened really carefully at the beginning of this book you heard me mention that Lake Moobegoners love their horseshoes. Folks around here toss them like they're goin' out of style but mostly it's a growed-up thing. Kids aren't involved because parents don't want them throwin' shoes until they're old enough to control the toss. I didn't start throwin' till I was 15. For most young boys it's a rite of passage.

Back in '85 the folks at Fender Brothers IGA Grocery got a right-near brilliant idea. Summer produce sales were slow so the Fenders condensed their produce section back, cleared out a 40-foot strip for two horseshoe pits and two concrete throwin' boxes and started a horseshoe league. Right in Aisle 1.

Seemed strange at first even to think about it, chunks of steel flyin' through the air and loud clanks goin' on by the Pop-Tarts. The genius in their decision wasn't apparent until after they'd gotten the pits put in. Men started coming every night. Ken Fender told me pop, juice and snack sales shot up 87 percent after the horseshoe pit installation.

Occasionally a shoe would clank the stake, fly in the air and land in a shopping cart but it didn't happen much. The worst thing I ever did hear was when an errant toss flattened a Captain Crunch display in Aisle 2. The kid was too young and shouldn't have been allowed to toss.

The day "Fender Brothers IGA & Indoor Horseshoe Toss" opened was a special day and not just because of the good weather. Ken Fender pulled a *coup de Moobegon* and got the famous Ottie Reno Horseshoe Family from Waverly, Ohio, to make the trip to show off their live horseshoe demonstration. (I drove in from Cincinnati with my wife Sue Ann just special for it.)

I first saw Ottie Reno at The Bob Evans Farms Festival in Rio Grande, Ohio. (In Ohio, Rio rhymes with Ohio.) He has to be well over 60 by now but he's still the world's best horseshoe pitcher, even won the Ohio State Championships and his family members don't lag far behind. They had this one trick where Ottie's daughter stood on her head between the pits, spread her legs and Ottie tossed perfect ringers over and between her legs.

The day the Renos showed was the most photographed day in Lake Moobegon history. Besides the usual *News Democrat* reporter we even had one from *Sports Illustrated*, yes, THE *Sports Illustrated* because they were curious about our grocery/indoor horseshoe combo from a letter they had received from the Lake Moobegon town clerk, Elsie Stanton. (They canned whatever story they were going to do after Ken Fender learned from Brian The Head Teller that they had an annual swimsuit issue in which women dress up like floozies. Ken got so mad he asked the guy to leave. In an interview with the *News Democrat*, Ken said he couldn't imagine him lettin' his daughter appear in a floozie rag like that.)

By the time Ottie drove up everybody had all but forgotten Ken Fender's blow-up. Ottie was the story. We all hooted and hollered as his bus pulled in because we had royalty in our midst. He was The Pete Rose of Horseshoes. It was a festive atmosphere: red, white, and blue bunting decorated the grocery all over; funny clowns filled helium balloons and the kids were inhalin' them to sound like Tattoo from Fantasy Island. Ken had the Methodists churn up homemade vanilla ice cream but no lemony sherbet. Ottie must have signed 250 autographs.

The real kick came when a select few of us got to go inside to watch the Reno Family dedicate the horseshoe pits. (Sue Ann and I were let in because of my brother's connection to Billy Fender.) And inside if Ottie didn't do that trick with his daughter! There she was, standin' on her head, legs spread and Ottie was throwin' ringer after ringer onto the stake that sat next to the Pop-Tarts. I thought I'd died and gone to horseshoe heaven.

And then it happened. Ottie Reno made Sue Ann the talk of Lake Moobegon. (You have to understand, folks in Lake Moobegon took a while warmin' up to Sue Ann, bein' she was an outsider.)

Here was how it went: While Ottie was explainin' a neat trick they planned on doin', he just up and pointed at Sue Ann and asked her if she could help. Sakes alive! Caught me by surprise. Ottie grabbed her by the arm and told her to lay on her back near the far pit by the Quaker Oatmeal, just three foot from the stake, which she did, then he jammed a foot-long candle in her mouth, lit the wick and stepped back. The flame flickered.

I got nervous.

It didn't take a brain surgeon to figure out ol' Ottie was goin' to throw a shoe from 40-feet, try to snuff out the flame and land a ringer. Anything short of 40 and my Sue Ann was good for dental work.

The first toss went well. The shoe grazed the wick, snuffed the flame, clanked the stake, *clank*. Applause. Then Ottie got this odd look, took out his tape measure and measured off the distance from Sue Ann to the end of the aisle.

He scratched his chin. "Thirty-nine feet," he said so everyone could hear.

He stuck a finger in the air, gauged the wind direction — of course there wasn't any indoors. After a couple knee bends, three jumpin' jacks, he cracked his knuckles — everybody turned away and went "Ugh" — and took a deep breath. He said, "I'm going to try something a little different today."

Meanwhile, candle wax was drippin' all over Sue Ann's cheek, her face was beet red and her eyes riveted to the flame like it was going to kill her if it stayed lit a moment longer. I felt for her.

"I'm goin' to throw the first ever over-the-shoulder-looking-into-a-mirror-facing-the-other-direction throw in the history of trick horseshoes."

Sue Ann gagged; her eyes got wide as a ping pong ball.

I sensed her fear and ran over to hold her hand. "You gonna make it, honey?"

"Pway."

"What you say?"

She lifted the candle out of her mouth and spat out melted candle wax. "Pray," she said.

I squeezed her hand and went back to my chair. She was real brave. The Twenty-Third Psalm seemed like a nice choice to start off a prayer, so I began where it says, "Though I walk through the valley of the shadow of death..."

Ottie pulled out a makeup kit mirror from his pocket. The crowd gasped. I ran both my hands through my hair. Sweat poured off Sue Ann's brow like rain to a tin roof. From a bag nearby Ol' Ottie took out a shiny red horseshoe, not a rubber horseshoe like he had been using, but a metal one. "Never used this kind before," he said. The *News Democrat* reporter looked like he was going to throw up.

I never thought Ottie Reno would miss but he did. Ottie's over-the-shoulder throw went in a high arc, cameras flashed like crazy, the shoe grazed the flourescent lights, more cameras flashed, and then it flew right over Sue Ann, missed the candle by inches and clanked the pole for a ringer anywat, *clank*. The crowd went nuts. I thought I was goin' to die of a heart attack.

A picture of Sue Ann with the shoe flyin' over her head ended up in the *News Democrat*. From that moment on Lake Moobegon accepted Sue Ann. A Lake Moobegon Church of Christ woman, Pete Cordray's wife, put her on par with Andy Holbrook and his 17 homers although I wouldn't have gone that far.

She'd been good but not that good. It was her faith that had pulled her through.

130

TWENTY

Lake Moobegon doesn't get its name from all the cows in southern Ohio because, for one, there aren't many cows in southern Ohio. It's all row crops and tobacco. Alverna the Assistant discovered the truth behind the town's name by accident in 1967 when she flipped open her grandmother's Bible that had been in the attic since the Civil War and out fell the evidence.

Apparently a Frenchman, Pierre Moux, had been a fur trapper back in the early 1700s and being the egotist he was he named the area around what is now Lake Moobegon as Lake Moux. This confounded Alverna the Assistant when she read it because there isn't a lake anywhere near Lake Moobegon today.

When she read further she learned that a great earthquake had hit the town in 1798 and swallowed up what was then a very large lake. The newest white settlers, mostly English and Scots-Irish, who were by then used to calling the area Lake Moux, began calling it Lake Moux-be-gone as a joke. The name stuck. To avoid having it pronounced Moocks-be-gon, the town fathers officially changed the spelling of the name to Lake Moobegon in 1823, thus retaining the original French pronunciation and making it easier to spell.

APPENDIX

One day Sue Ann and I will own a coal stove like the one Grandma Renie has so I can tell our kids the same stories she told me. Coal stoves are nice because they give off good heat and coal is pretty cheap. There's nothin' like openin' that black iron door, stokin' the flame, and tossin' in another chunk while the heat roars out to scorch your eyebrows.

I have more stories to share with you. Shoot, I've heard enough stories just from the men at the Cyclone Store to write a full-length novel or another "War and Peace." All the real-old story tellers in Lake Moobegon used to sit down at the Cyclone Store to swap yarns. My great-great uncle Squeezie hung out there in the '40s.

Thanks for lettin' me share the heart and soul of Lake Moobegon, Ohio. If you really enjoyed my yarns just drop me a line. That way when the next book prints I'll let you know in advance so you can buy it to help me pay off the debt I incurred from writing this one.

With love.

— Danny Talbott • Box 154 Vernon Center MN 56090

[About the Author: Daniel J. Vance lives in Vernon Center, Minn., with his wife Carolyn, and children Abigail and Patrick. He is the editor of Connect Business Magazine. He has also written and published "William 'Bill' Carlson: The Founder of Carlson Craft" and "Sal: The Autobiography of Sal Frederick."]